The Garden of the
Villa Mollini
and other stories

The Garden of the Villa Mollini
and other stories

by
ROSE TREMAIN

Hamish Hamilton · London

For my Mother, Jane Thomson,
with love.

462762

First published in Great Britain 1987
by Hamish Hamilton Ltd
27 Wrights Lane, London W8 5TZ
Copyright © 1987 by Rose Tremain

Some of the stories in this collection first appeared in the
following publications: 'Will and Lou's Boy', *Paris Review*,
Summer 1985; 'The Garden of the Villa Mollini', *Critical
Quarterly*, January 1987; 'Tropical Fish', *Listener*, July 1985;
'La Plume de Mon Ami', *Foreign Exchange*, ed. Julian
Evans, Hamish Hamilton and Abacus, 1985; 'Wildtrack',
Winter's Tales: New Series 2, ed. Robin Baird-Smith,
Constable, 1986; 'The Kite Flyer', *The Seven Deadly Sins*,
Severn House, 1984; and 'The Bellows of the Fire', *Good
Housekeeping*, 1987.

British Library Cataloguing in Publication Data

Tremain, Rose
The garden of the Villa Mollini and other stories.
I. Title
823'.914[F]   PR6070.R364
ISBN 0–241–12075–6

Typeset by
Katerprint Typesetting Services, Oxford
Printed in Great Britain by
Butler & Tanner Ltd, Frome and London

Contents

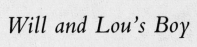

Will and Lou's Boy

THIS WAS AN average dawn in the early summer of 1948, the year I got to be eighteen.

'Eat your fishcake, Dougie,' said Lou.

They were barracouta fishcakes. Awful. They tasted like it was the fish's seaweedy liver you were eating.

'Yes, eat your fishcake, Doug,' said Will.

Will and Lou. I thought of them as one: *Willou*. I was their son, Douglas. I was their only child.

Chief in our household was Lou's obsession to win the Queen Mary Gardening Cup. In 1947, we'd entered for the Princess Royal Gardening Cup, but we hadn't won it and Lou had turned her disappointment into rage. Until then, she'd been a moderately contented woman. Now, she was raging and cooking barracouta. Poor Will. Poor me. The world was funny those years.

We had a pre-fab. They'd built the row we were on in about one day. Only pre-fab dwellers were allowed to enter for the gardening cups. Rain had knocked down a lot of Lou's gladioli the night before Cup Day. It hadn't rained in Wandsworth, where the winner lived, and this was one among lots of things that didn't seem fair to Lou. 'Soddin' Wandsworth!' she'd say. She never normally swore much. She'd learnt 'soddin' from my Aunt If, who'd learnt it from my Uncle Pepino who sold ice-cream and illegal nylons meant for export. My Uncle Pepino was Italian, but pretended not to be during the war. 'Call me Pep,' he'd ask. 'Yes, call him Peppy,' said Aunt If, who, at the age of sixteen, had rebaptized herself Iphigenia. Her old name, which my father still used sometimes, was Gladys. She could get as angry about being called Gladys as Lou could get about Wandsworth. The men in our family, including me, seem to be calmer people than the women. Peppy was arrested that year, but he stayed calm.

The best thing about dawn in that pre-fab was knowing you'd be out of it all day. We were all out, even Lou, who worked in a rayon factory. Will was a wireless assembler. He had the same reverence for wirelesses as some people have for God. He relied on the Home Service to tell him who or what he was. He'd polish our wireless, this fount of understanding, with Min Cream and old stockings. Lou said a man like him ought to have a secure future. And she'd look at me. Sometimes, this sideways look of hers made me think she was thinking I didn't have a future of any kind, let alone secure. Lou and Will. Will and Lou. *Willou.*

I was a park attendant. My wage was four pound ten a week, not bad for then. Bits of my park had been ploughed up and sown with barley. This barley spoilt the atmosphere of the park, made it somehow noisier. Also, the kids used the barley to piss in. I'd see the heads of the girls, squatted down. But despite or notwithstanding the barley, I loved that park. That year, all the benches were getting painted and the fishpond was restocked with gold-fish. We had a new Head of Parks called Mr. Dowdswell, who wasn't like a clerk, but more like a visionary. The day they ploughed up his lawns for cereal, he developed the habit of tugging out hanks of his hair.

For my eighteenth birthday, Lou said, 'You ask a friend, Dougie.' I didn't have any friends really, as Lou perfectly well knew, so I asked Knacky Mick, who sold matches and empty boxes and tins of bootblack on the corner by my park gates. Knacky Mick was a Wicklow son, blue-pale in that way only the Irish are in winter. He must have been fifty. 'I'm an orphan, you know, Doug,' he often said. I liked him. When he heard I had an uncle getting black market stuff, he began to take an interest in me and sneak me matches for Lou, 'For the gas fire, like.' We

4

didn't have a gas fire in the pre-fab. We didn't have a fire at all, but a paraffin heater Lou christened Old Smoky. But Lou liked getting matches. She grew to expect it. Free anything, in those peculiar days, was appreciated – a rubber band, a safety pin, a half yard of knicker elastic . . . and one afternoon, Lou won second prize in a raffle, one solitary brown egg. The first prize was three bananas. Lou didn't complain. She scrambled the egg with a lot of milk and we shared it on toast. She dreamt about the bananas, though. She dreamt someone gave us a banana tree for the pre-fab garden.

Two things were coming: the party for my eighteenth birthday and the day of judgment in the Queen Mary Gardening Cup. There was a long heatwave. The barley in my park started to ripen. Courting couples began the habit of lying down in it and I was supposed to shoo them away. 'I'm sorry, Sir, I'm afraid you're spoiling our crop,' Mr. Dowdswell told me to say. One day, I said by mistake, 'I'm sorry, Sir, I'm afraid you're *soiling* our crop,' and I was so miserable at getting the wrong word, I left the couples alone after that, and the barley, which had once been a kids' lavatory, now became a field of iniquity.

The most iniquitous person in our family was my cousin, Patricia, daughter of Aunt If and Peppy the Italian. In the war, she'd fallen in love with a G.I. called Wedderburn C. Wicklens, a Southern, beefy man, raised with his gut full of corn pone and his brain full of cotton. He was from Louisiana State. Patricia could just imagine the kind of wooden house she'd own on the New Orleans delta, and when Wicklens left her in '46, she cried herself almost into the grave. Now, two years later, Wedderburn C. Wicklens was back and cousin Pat was made a bride. Peppy's son-in-law was exactly one foot and four inches taller than him, as witnessed to this day by the wedding photograph. In this picture, everyone's grinning except me. I'm standing to attention. 'God!' Lou sometimes used to say, staring at the photo on Aunt If's tiled mantlepiece, 'just look at that nincompoop!'

Preparing our garden for the Cup and preparing for this grand meal we'd have when I was eighteen took a lot of

5

resourcefulness. We nicked bricks from the bomb site on Weatherby Road to make a garden 'wall' that never got higher than two feet. I nicked bedding antirrhinums and nemesia from the park and stakes for the gladioli, over which Lou was taking no chances. I would have got the sack if Mr. Dowdswell had caught me, but Mr. Dowdswell was a man who saw vistas of things, not small transactions. Uncle Peppy, not yet in prison, figured big in our planning, so did Wicklens, whom we now addressed as 'Wed.' 'In more than one sense Wed,' I said. But no one laughed. 'Shame Dougie was too young to see Combat,' I heard Wed say to Lou one evening. 'Yes,' she said, 'it might have been the saving of him.'

They thought being eighteen might be the saving of me. If we could just scrimp together enough ration cards, if Peppy could just do a nylons deal with the butcher, if Wed could just get whisky and chocolate powder and margarine from the PX, if If could just run me up a new tweed jacket. If, if, if. . . . 'You'll feel better when you're eighteen, Dougie,' Lou lullabyed as she tucked me in. 'You'll feel more like a man.' So I lay and thought about this. I didn't think I'd grow up like Will – to be good. I knew I wouldn't grow up like Peppy – to be smart. When I imagined my future, it was exactly the same as my present. The only thing that changed wasn't me but the park. They harvested the dirty barley. They ploughed in the stubble and back into the soil went the sweet papers and the used johnnies and the hairpins, and the land was resown with grass and everything in the park became orderly again. Mr. Dowdswell's hair grew back. We were allocated some new shears. The thing I wanted to say to Lou was, 'I'm not unhappy.'

Then we heard about the housing lottery.

The coming of the news about the housing lottery was like the coming of malaria. Lou began to sweat. It was like the jungle had suddenly surrounded her. She'd fan the air with her knitting patterns. 'You can't breathe in this place,' she'd say, making our barracouta cakes. 'Help your mother,' Will would say accusingly. So I'd set the table and get out the tea strainer and stare at Lou's arms, white and moist above the greasy pan. Love for Lou has always been something I've suffered from. Even in my imagined future, I still suffered from it. 'I don't mind the pre-fab,' I'd say to Lou's arms preparing our seaweed meal. Without looking up at me, she'd say, 'Don't be silly, Douglas.'

It was me they sent to get our lottery number. The Housing Office had women queuing right down the stairs and into the street. I missed an entire afternoon's work standing in that queue, risking my job for Lou's malaria. 'You're not eligible if you've got a pre-fab, love,' someone told me, but I hung on. There must have been a thousand people there, not counting babies, two thousand upper and lower jaws all wagging about hardship and eligibility and fairness. Our number was 879. Aunt If said this was auspicious because 879 was a close-together group of numbers. I thought of the number as representing our family. I was the thin 7 in the middle, with Lou and Will leaning over me. Even now – and they're both long dead, actually – I still sometimes think of Lou as 8 and Will as 9. 'Dear God, please take care of the immortal souls of 8 and 9,' I sometimes pray. And I feel them at my side, Will watching me, Lou with her profile turned.

A lot happened the following day. Mr. Dowdswell gave me a Severe Reprimand, Knacky Mick was taken to hospital, and Uncle Pepino was arrested for illegal trading. Aunt If, who is something of a gypsy to look at, read catastrophe in the stars, pawned her sewing machine to raise Peppy's bail, and cried on Lou's shoulder. 'At least,' said Lou to her sister-in-law, 'you've still got your own house.' I left them and got a bus to the hospital. Our lottery ticket was stuck up on the mantlepiece behind a glass unicorn. Knacky Mick, when I found him, was Irish-blue under his stubble and dosed to his skull. 'Suppressing me, they are,' he muttered. In his locker were his match-boxes and his tins of shoeblack, piled up. 'Come to a party,' I said, 'I'd like to invite you to my eighteenth birthday party.'

'Very good,' he said.

I didn't mind the hospital. I sat by Knacky Mick for quite a while. A drip was hitched up to his vein. Other patients winked at me, the ones on their own without visitors. Knacky Mick slept a drugged sleep. The room was high and light and full of people whispering. It wouldn't be bad, I thought, working here. This was the first time I ever imagined having a job quite far away from Will and Lou. It gave me an odd feeling, as if I'd made myself an orphan.

Now, four things were coming: the Gardening Cup, my eighteenth birthday party, Pepino's trial and the housing lottery. No wonder Lou couldn't breathe. These things were like weights on her chest. My ideal future was one in which there was nothing to fear and nothing to hope for. I didn't mind if we got chocolate powder for my party or not. I didn't care if we went to live in a new flat with a refrigerator or not. 'The trouble with Dougie,' said my cousin Pat, dreaming still of her Louisiana clapboard house, 'is he's got no imagination.' Well, I didn't care if I had imagination or not either. The thing that was awful was that Lou had started to care so much about everything, she seemed deranged. And I cared about that. I wanted her to be like she'd been when she'd won the solitary egg – contented.

Our pre-fab garden looked neat on Cup Day. We'd stuck in the shearings from a conifer hedge in my park, to look like a new little conifer hedge. We took down our washing line. Mr. Dowdswell let me borrow the edging shears to straighten up the grass. It wasn't bad. The adjudicator smiled at Lou's new home perm and said, 'Very nice. Congratulations.' Under the perm, her malaria was still raging away. 'It means a lot to us,' she said, in a choked voice. And the adjudicator took off his look of admiration and put on a look of pity and I knew we hadn't won.

'We haven't won, Louie,' I told her.

'You know nothing about anything, Douglas,' she told me back. Which, in a way, was true.

Wedderburn Wicklens gave me forty Senior Service cigarettes on the day of my birthday. I didn't smoke, so I gave them to Willou, who did. I thought how odd it was that Wed hadn't noticed I didn't smoke. But there were a lot of things Wed didn't notice, like for instance, he quite often called Patricia 'Candice.' 'If you call me Candice again, I'll kill you!' she once told him. But this threat of death didn't seem to do the trick. Half way through my eighteenth birthday meal, a huge belch rumbled up out of his stomach and he said quickly: 'didn't hear that, did you, Candy honey?' 'Who's Candy?' asked Willou simultaneously. Patricia slammed down her knife and fork and ran out into the hot night falling. Pepino stood up. Beside my gypsy Aunt If, he looked like a little yellow duck. '*You!*' he yelled. 'You mind! You Yanki-panki!' And then he sat down again and Wed got up and wandered lazily out to Patricia.

We were eating pork ribs, for which Pepino had paid four pairs of nylons. Our fingers and chins were mucky and red from Lou's sauce of boiled tomatoes. Wed told us we should call this meal *spare*ribs and Will guffawed with derision, 'Typical American!' he said, 'call everything superfluous!' We picked the last shreds of meat from the ribs and washed these pickings down with beer. Lou had got her chocolate powder and her egg powder and on the afternoon she was told the winner of the Queen Mary Gardening Cup lived in Camberwell, she cried away her hopes into an enormous cake. She wrote (she hadn't got a fantastic imagination either) D 18 on the top with angelica she'd bought before the war. It made me uneasy. I thought, I'm glad she couldn't tattoo it onto me.

Knacky Mick never came to my birthday party, he was too ill. I saved him some cake. I thought, I've only got one friend and that's Knacky Mick and he's going to snuff it. I felt a bit like crying, but Lou and Will had their eye on me. Full of beer, they said, 'This is a new start, Dougie. This is your chance to start again.' I started to say I was perfectly content as I was, but nobody was actually listening. Will and Lou and Peppy and If had turned away from me and were lighting up the Senior Service I'd given them and talking about their chances of being rehoused, in Peppy's case in Brixton jail and in Willou's case in William Petrie Buildings, the lotteried flats with fridges and radiators. I looked round to see what was happening to Pat and Wed

9

and I saw them kissing by the conifer hedge. I unwrapped the bobble hat Lou had knitted for my birthday present and put it on. The thought that Lou's fingers had fashioned every one of the stitches that went round and round my head made me feel very warm and happy. 'Just look at him!' she said a while later, blowing smoke at Peppy, '*Honestly!*'

On the morning of the housing lottery, Lou couldn't face cooking barracouta, so we had bread and jam for breakfast. Will turned on the Home Service to calm his wife's beating heart. I left as early as I could to walk to my park and it was a beautiful morning, still and shiny and the smell of the park in summer was as fantastic to me as the smell of the Majestic cinema was to Lou. A consignment of bedding geraniums had arrived, and I started to dig over the bed where they'd go in. I tried not to think about 879, or about Lou waiting with thousands of other women to hear the numbers called out. There were fifty-one flats in William Petrie Buildings and at least twenty times that number of applicants. Mr. Dowdswell came by to look at the geraniums. 'Good work, Douglas,' he said approvingly, and then tapped my bending back and said in his confidential stammer: 'No more bla . . . no more yer bloody barley next year, thank Ga . . . thank God!' 'Hooray, Sir.' I answered.

When I got home, Lou was resting and Will was mushing up the barracouta we hadn't eaten for breakfast. 'Don't disturb your mother,' said Will.

'We didn't get one, did we?' I said.

'No,' said Will.

I went to wash my hands at the sink. Outside, the stuck-in conifers were going brown.

'869 was lucky,' said Will, 'and 849 and 859, but not 879. Shame we had the 7.'

I stared at Will and then beyond him to the bedroom where Lou was lying in the aftermath of her malaria. *Willou.* 8 and 9. Without me, they would have got lucky. I was the 7 alright. I'd made them lose.

That August Knacky Mick died and I applied for a job at the hospital where I'd visited him and where I've been now all my life. I told Willou this was my new start, and they were proud of me. But my last day at the park was one of the saddest things I can remember. They'd harvested the barley. I sat in the sunshine, staring at all the litter left among the stubble and thinking about my country.

The Garden of
the Villa Mollini

BEFORE THE ARRIVAL of Antonio Mollini in 1877, the villa had been called, simply, the Villa Bianca, the White House. It came to be known as the Villa Mollini, not through the vanity of Antonio Mollini himself, but through the pride of the people of the village. They wanted to be able to say – to travellers who passed that way, to relations who journeyed there from Arezzo or Rapolano or Assisi – 'We have in our midst the great Mollini, the world's most renowned opera singer. He knows us and even remembers the names of our children.'

In fact, Antonio Mollini was seldom there. He was forty-one when he bought the villa and his voice had entered what the critics later termed its 'decade of magnificence'. His life was passed in the musical capitals of Europe — Milan, Paris, Vienna. He came to the Villa Mollini only to rest, to visit his wife and to plan his garden.

He wanted, in the design of this garden, to express a simple and optimistic philosophy. He believed that his life was a journey of discovery, revelation and surprise and that it led forward perpetually, never back. In it, there was not merely one goal, one destination, but many, each one leading forwards from the next. All were different. Repetition seldom, if ever, occurred. He would not allow it to occur. And even at life's close, he thought there would be new landscapes and new visions of hope. The garden he was going to create would thus be infinitely varied, intricate and above all beautiful.

15

It was fortunate, then, that the terrain on which he would realise the garden wasn't flat, but sloped gently upwards away from the house to a cypress grove, and then descended, equally gently, towards a river. On the other side of the river, there were clover fields and, beyond these, a forest. The far edge of the forest was the boundary of Mollini's land.

His head gardener, Paulo Pappavincente, was the illegitimate son of a priest. Pappavincente's mother had died at his birth and he'd been brought up by aged and devout grandparents unable to conceal their shame at his existence. Though Mollini explained his philosophy carefully to Pappavincente, using simple terms, baby language almost, the gardener was unable to see life as his master saw it. To him, it led, repetitively and inevitably, to dark and deep abysses of guilt. But he didn't want to bore Mollini or anger him with chatter about his own sufferings; he wanted to design the most beautiful garden in Tuscany, so that one day he could say to his own legitimate grandchildren, 'I made it. I made the garden of the Villa Mollini.' He did suggest, however, that a well be sunk at a certain place, not far from the house, where Mollini had thought a statue of the goddess Diana would draw the eye forward. 'I think a well also beckons, Sir,' he said. To his surprise and also to his relief, Mollini agreed. That night, as he knelt to say his prayers, Pappavincente began to feel that good fortune was stealing into his life.

The same night, Antonio Mollini's wife, Rosa, stared by candlelight at the half-completed sketches of the box aisles and the fountains, the herbarium and the rose trellises, the steps and terraces leading up to the cypress grove and down to the river, and said aloud, 'I think he must contrive a lake.'

Mollini was asleep. He lay on his back, snoring, with his legs apart. From his magnificent lungs came an unmelodious kind of squealing. Rosa pulled aside the curtains of the bed and leaned over him, holding her candle.

'Antonio,' she whispered, 'please, Antonio.'

He opened his eyes. This thin white face of Rosa's on its

16

pale neck sometimes reminded him of a sad mask on a stick.

'What, Rosa?'

'When the river leaves our land, westwards, where does it arrive, Antonio?'

'In the village.'

'Then I expect we may have to move the village.'

Mollini stared up. He chose his mistresses for their roundness, for their bright colour. Rosa was his little ghostly possession.

'We cannot move the village, Rosa.'

Tears sparkled in her eyes.

'Please, Antonio. You must make a lake.'

Pappavincente was consulted. When he heard of the plan to dam up the river, he descended once more into his habitual pessimism. Politely, he informed his master of the life-sustaining properties of the village water supply. Antonio Mollini felt ashamed. He loved the village people. He'd made a list of all their names and the names of their children so that he wouldn't forget them, and now, in the night, he'd allowed his wife to suggest something that would impoverish and destroy them. 'Rosa is mad', he said to Pappavincente, 'but forgive her. Since the death of Pietro, her mind often wanders astray.'

The death of Pietro had occurred in the same year that Mollini's fame was born. Consumption thus played a role in both events. As Mollini sang Alfredo in Verdi's *La Traviata*, his son Pietro was dying of Violetta's disease. He refused to mourn. He looked at the little coffin. He would have more sons. He would replace Pietro. He would christen all his sons 'Pietro', so that if another one died, he, too, could be replaced. Rosa accused him of callousness. 'No,' he said, 'but I will not let death win.'

Rosa didn't conceive. She knew that loss, like starvation, can make a woman barren. She would be barren for ever, mourning Pietro. She longed, at that time, for a garden. She thought it would make her feel more kindly towards the world if she could bury seeds in the earth and see leaves emerge, bright green. But Mollini wasn't yet

17

rich. They lived in Milan in a narrow house on a dark courtyard. The Villa Mollini was six years away.

In those six years, Pappavincente fathered four sons, one of whom he christened Pietro.

Mollini fathered none. His fame grew. 'There is no adequate epithet to describe Mollini's voice,' one French critic wrote. 'To say it is like honey, or like velvet, or like silver is merely to debase it. It is like no other voice we have ever heard.'

On its gentle hillside, the Villa Mollini, still known as the Villa Bianca and occupied by a professor of medicine, waited for the great man's arrival.

In the week following Rosa's dreadful request for a lake, Mollini left for Milan. On his forty-second birthday, the day he began rehearsals for La Scala's new production of Wagner's *Tristan und Isolde*, he met for the first time the internationally known soprano, Verena Dusa, and fell in love with her.

La Dusa was thirty-four. Her elbows were dimpled and her belly and breasts round and firm and fat. She was the mistress of the impresario, Riccardo Levi, from whose bed Mollini quickly wooed her.

Riccardo Levi demanded a duel and was refused. He threatened to ruin La Dusa's career, but his threats were ignored. La Dusa moved her dresses and her fan collection from Levi's apartment to Mollini's town house. In despair, Riccardo Levi wrote a letter to Rosa, telling Mollini's wife that she had been betrayed.

Rosa examined the letter. She held it near to her face because her eyesight was getting bad and Riccardo Levi had small, mean handwriting. As she read the word 'betrayed', she felt a pain shoot down from her knees to the soles of her feet, as if in seconds she'd become an old crone, unable to walk. She put the letter down and stood up, clinging first to the writing table, then to the wall. She went to the window. A team of surveyors had arrived. Pappavincente was describing to them an imaginary circle, the site of his well. Rosa tapped on the window, to summon Pappavincente to help her, but her tap was too feeble and he couldn't hear her. Her maid came in a while later and found her lying on the floor. She was unable to speak. Her maid called for help. Rosa was put to bed and a doctor sent for. With the arrival of the doctor, word spread to Pappavincente and the other gardeners that the Signora was ill. Retribution, thought Pappavincente.

The doctor examined Rosa. She was in shock, he told the servants. Something must have frightened her – something she'd seen from the window, perhaps? The servants shrugged their shoulders. Rosa's maid stroked her mistress's cold white forehead. Keep her warm, said the doctor and went away. Coverlets were piled on the bed, one on top of another, so that the shape of Rosa's body disappeared completely beneath them and only her small head stuck out like a tiny sprout on a desirée potato.

She lay without speaking for a week. Her maid propped her up and spooned vermicelli broth into her narrow mouth. Outside her window, she could hear men talking and tried to turn her head to listen. 'Drains,' her maid explained gently, 'they're here to re-route the drains and lay conduits to the fountains.'

The doctor returned. His own wife quite often irritated him by succumbing to illnesses he was unable to cure except by cradling her in his arms like a baby. He looked at Rosa's blank face. He refused to cradle *her* in his arms. There were dark hairs on her top lip and creases in her eyelids. 'Where is Signor Mollini?' he snapped. 'He must be sent for.'

So the servants sent for the priest. He, too, came and stared at Rosa and placed a palm leaf cross on her coverlet mountain and then sat down, in the silence of her room, and wrote in exquisite calligraphy to Antonio Mollini, informing him that his wife appeared to be dying.

When the letter arrived in Milan, on an early morning of grey mist, Mollini's voice – that same voice that had caused thousands of Society women to weep with wonder behind their opera glasses – was whispering playful obscenities in La Dusa's ear. She squirmed and giggled and pouted and the pout of her wide lips was so delicious and irresistible that Mollini was unable to stop himself from kissing them again and murmuring through his nose, 'I love you, Verena. I love you beyond everything.'

His servant knocked at his door. He rolled over and covered La Dusa's breasts with the sheet. The servant excused himself and came forward to the bed and offered Mollini the priest's letter on a silver salver. It was written on fine parchment, like a communion wafer. Mollini snatched it up and told the servant not to disturb him again that morning. The servant bowed and retreated. Mollini glanced at the letter, tossed it onto the marble bedside cabinet and turned back to La Dusa who lay with her arms above her head, waiting for his embrace.

The letter was forgotten. He remembered it at last towards six o'clock that evening, as he was preparing to leave for the opera house. He opened it as he was gargling with blackcurrant cordial. When he read the word 'dying', he choked on the gargle and spat it all over the bathroom floor. He wiped his mouth, read the letter again and sat down on a stool. For the first time in several months, he remembered Pietro, and at once he saw, clearly and beautifully, where fate had led and where indeed it was leading. It was leading to La Dusa. Rosa was dying because she was unable to bear him more sons. It was fitting. Rosa was dried up, barren, old before her time. But here, right here in his bed, was Verena Dusa with her succulent round hips that would accommodate his future children. All he had to do was to marry her. It was gloriously simple. It was like stepping from a dark, shaded laurel walk onto a sunny terrace and finding at your feet pots of scented jasmine.

That same evening, Rosa spoke for the first time in seven days. She asked her maid to help her into the garden. When she crept out from under the coverlets, she seemed to have shrunk. Her long white nightgown was tangled round her feet. She looked like a chrysalis.

She was wrapped up in a cloak. Her hair was brushed and pinned up. She went hesitantly down the stairs, clinging to her maid's arm.

Pappavincente was standing in the garden in the twilight, looking at the well shafts. The water table was low.

The construction workers had sunk the shafts almost fifty feet. He looked up and saw Rosa totter out with her maid. 'Forgive her', Mollini had said. Pappavincente left the well and started to walk towards her. Her maid sat her down on a little stone seat. She stared about her in bewilderment. Deep trenches had been dug in the terraces. Mounds of red earth and lengths of lead piping lay all around.

'Signora,' said Pappavincente, bowing, 'for your recovery we are making all these waterworks.' But she only stared at him in bewilderment too, as if he were a lunatic, as if he were the village idiot. 'I want,' she said, looking at the devastation round her, 'my husband back.' Up above the chimneys of the house and above the garden several bats were circling. Rosa liked bats. 'Pipistrelli,' she'd call, 'pipi, pipi . . .'

Unaware that the priest had written to Mollini, Rosa that night had the lamp lit on her writing desk and sat down with her pen. She told Mollini that she had been ill and that she had imagined she was lying in a grave with Pietro. Over her body, the earth had been piled higher and higher in a colossal mound, with only her head sticking out. She could not, she said, endure such imaginings and only his love could save her from them. She would forgive him his sin of the flesh if he would just return to her. She signed the letter *Your Wife Until Death, Rosa Mollini*. Her writing, unlike the priest's hand, was cramped and ugly and her spelling not terribly good.

Rosa's letter reached Milan four days later. Mollini and La Dusa had triumphed in *Tristan und Isolde* and had been invited each night to elegant suppers by the likes of the Duke of Milan and the Count of Piedmont and had revelled together in their glory. At one of these suppers Mollini had become tottering drunk on a surfeit of champagne and pleasure and had rested his head on La Dusa's bosom and proposed marriage to her. The other guests had gasped, remembering the small, elegant wife he used to bring to evenings such as these, but La Dusa had only laughed and stroked his burning cheek and told him she was his till she died.

When he read Rosa's letter (he had a hangover when it

was brought to him and his head was throbbing) he knew that he wouldn't, *couldn't* go back to her. When he thought about his life with Rosa, he was amazed he'd been able to endure it for so many years. Because it seemed full of shadow. Only at Pietro's birth had the sun shone on it and after his death it had become colourless and ghostly.

But Mollini knew also that he couldn't abandon his plans for the garden to Rosa and Pappavincente, both of whose natures were pessimistic and depressive. So he decided he would take La Dusa back with him to the Villa Mollini. He was a great man, revered in the village. He could do as he liked. He was beyond criticism. And he wouldn't hide La Dusa away. Oh, no. He would move out of the rooms he'd shared with Rosa and into other rooms which he'd share with La Dusa. When they were invited out, both women would accompany him, wife and mistress. Tuscan society would be given the chance to exclaim upon La Dusa's gorgeous beauty. And Rosa? Rosa was a religious, reserved woman. She would behave piously, with dignity, staying away from him most of the time, reading or sewing in her rooms or going to communion.

Having obtained La Dusa's willing agreement to these arrangements, Mollini wrote to tell Rosa that he was returning home, but that he was unable to live without Verena Dusa and that she would therefore be coming with him.

Five days later, they arrived at the Villa Mollini to be told by the servants that Rosa was dead. She had been found with a burned scrap of paper in her hand, which they thought might have been a letter. She had shot herself with one of Mollini's duelling pistols.

Summer was coming. The re-routing of the drains wasn't entirely successful. As Mollini and his love sat with their fingers entwined on the first of the terraces to be completed, they fancied they could smell something decidedly unsavoury.

It had been a dry spring and the river was low. Verena Dusa went down and looked at the river and said, as she strolled along with her plump little hand fondling

Mollini's velvet-clad buttocks, 'You know what I would like here, my darling? A lake.'

Pappavincente was summoned. 'I am going to dam up the river,' Mollini informed him. 'Water will be taken to the village in metal containers. Every villager will have his rightful share.'

Pappavincente went down to the village, informed the people what was happening and told them to march shoulder to shoulder up to the Villa and break down the gates and threaten to kill Signor Mollini if he went ahead with his dam. 'We will!' said a few voices. 'We won't let our river be taken away!' And some of the men got out their pitchforks and their scythes. But nearly all the women of the village folded their arms and shrugged their shoulders. 'As long as we have water,' they said, 'we're really perfectly happy. Perhaps it will be less trouble to get water from the containers than from the river. And anyway, we mustn't forget how lucky we are to have Signor Mollini right here in our valley . . .'

They could see, however, that Pappavincente was in despair. They comforted him. 'You're adding to the fame of this region with your wonderful garden,' they told him, 'and a lake will make it even better. You must put swans on it, Pappavincente, and graceful boats.'

So Pappavincente walked back up to the Villa with not one villager standing with him, shoulder to shoulder. He thought he would sell his cottage and take his wife and sons and leave Mollini for ever. But then he let himself into the garden by a side gate and stood and stared at one of the new fountains and at the water lilies he'd planted at its base and thought of all the work still to be done, and he knew that, if he left the garden, he'd regret it till he died. It was his one work of art.

Mollini had understood the look of agony on Pappavincente's face. He was relieved he'd thought up the idea of taking water to the villagers in containers, because he knew that if La Dusa wanted a lake, he would have to give her a lake. He was much too afraid of losing her to deny her anything. Indeed, he begged her, begged her on his knees with his arms round her thighs to ask of him whatever she wanted, no matter how costly, no matter how perverse. All he longed to do was to give, to give.

She laughed at him. He adored her laugh, It made him tremble with delight. 'You can give me a wedding ring, Antonio!' she giggled.

He'd thought, after burying Rosa, that he would wait six months before marrying Verena. It seemed right to wait. But it was clear to him as the summer advanced that La Dusa would insist on being married before new opera commitments began for them both in September. Hardly a day went by now without her asking, 'Will it be August, Antonio?'

So he decided he wouldn't wait six months. He set a date: August 17th. He wanted the dam completed by then and a chapel built at the lake's edge, where the wedding would take place. More builders were hired. The same priest who had written to Mollini on Rosa's behalf was now given money to consecrate the ground on which the chapel was going to stand. An order was sent to Lake Trasimeno for forty-two swans. A fat ruby, encircled with diamonds, was placed on La Dusa's finger. Invitations went out to all the important people in the opera world – patrons and practitioners, both – and rooms booked for them in every inn and hostelry for miles around.

Then in July, as the dam was finished and the river went dry and the first containers of water rolled in on carts to the village, Mollini fell ill. He started vomiting. Pain in his bowel made him curse in agony. He had a terrible fever.

The doctor came. He took off his tail coat and rolled up his shirtsleeves and gave Mollini an enema. The contents of the bowel were putrified, he noticed, greenish and foul. 'Advanced colonic infection,' he diagnosed and arranged for Mollini to be taken that night to a hospital in Siena.

La Dusa travelled in the carriage with him. His face, normally ruddy and healthy, looked grey. He was suffering. La Dusa wiped his forehead with a little lace handkerchief. She was petrified. Supposing he died before the wedding?

When they reached the hospital, Mollini appeared to be delirious, not knowing where he was. As they went in through a heavy, iron-studded door, La Dusa held her lace handkerchief to her nostrils. The stench of the place was appalling. Every breath she breathed seemed to her to be full of poison. And though it was night-time, it was a stupidly rowdy place. Doors slammed, nurses marched up and down the echoing corridors in stalwart shoes, patients cried out, gas lamps hissed, cleaning women in filthy aprons pushed iron slop buckets forward on the stone floors with their mops.

La Dusa felt sick. How could anyone be made well in such a place? As Mollini was carried in, they passed a flight of stairs leading downwards. TO THE MORGUE, said a sign. The sign was accompanied by a drawing of a hand with a pointing finger. La Dusa couldn't help noticing that the drawing of the hand was very fine, like a drawing by da Vinci or Michelangelo. This must be where their talents lie, she thought – in the direction of death.

Mollini was put into an iron bed in the middle of a long ward. La Dusa protested, but no one listened and they were left quite alone. All along the row, men were groaning and sighing. A nurse came in. She passed briskly down the line of groaning patients, barely glancing at any of them. La Dusa stood up. She took her handkerchief away from her nose, drew in a breath and then let out a high F Sharp with extraordinary force.

The nurse stopped in her tracks and stared at her with a look of utter incredulity. Several of the patients woke from sleep and raised their heads.

La Dusa heard herself shout at the nurse, 'Do you know who this is? This is Antonio Mollini! Why has he been put here?'

'This is the Men's Ward, Signora.'

'And why is there no surgeon? Is this what you do to your patients – put them in a line and forget them?'

'Of course we don't forget them.'

'I want Signor Mollini moved to a quiet room and I want a surgeon called now!'

The nurse gave La Dusa a dirty look and stomped out of the ward. La Dusa returned to Mollini's bed and stared at him. His eyes were closed and his breathing shallow. She was glad, in a way, that he couldn't see the terrible ward or hear or smell the sufferings of the other men. She stroked his hand. 'I will fight for you, my love,' she said.

After half an hour, the nurse returned. 'There is no surgeon here at the moment,' she said sourly. 'Surgeons need rest, you know. But if you can pay, we can have Signor Mollini moved to a more secluded room.'

'Pay?' said La Dusa, 'Of course we can pay!'

Mollini was lifted onto a stretcher and carried out of the ward. He was put into another iron bed in a tiny room, like a cell. A chair was brought to La Dusa and she sat down. They told her that one of the surgeons had woken up and would come and look at Mollini as soon as he had cleaned his teeth.

The door of the little cell was shut. Alone with Mollini's sufferings, La Dusa felt so frightened that she began to cry. Her tears were very bright and copious and the little lace handkerchief was soon saturated with them.

When the surgeon arrived, she was still weeping. The surgeon wore a silk cravat. He shook her hand, that was wet from holding the handkerchief. She gave him a scribbled note from Mollini's doctor. When he'd read it, he lifted up the covers and began to prod Mollini's belly.

The surgeon's hand on his bowel caused terrible pain. Mollini's eyes opened and rolled about and he choked in agony. The face of the surgeon became grave. La Dusa wiped her wet hand on her skirt and knelt by Mollini, holding him and kissing his face as the surgeon's fingers probed.

The surgeon replaced Mollini's covers and put his hands together in a kind of steeple under his chin. 'We must open him up,' he said.

He was taken away. La Dusa was told to wait in the tiny room. She lay on the bed and tried to doze, but her own anxiety and the unceasing noise of the hospital prevented sleep. The short night passed and a grey light seeped in through the tiny window.

At seven, Mollini was brought in on a stretcher and put back into the bed. He was unconscious and pale as death. The surgeon, too, looked pale and there was sweat on his

26

top lip. 'I'm afraid,' he said, 'the decay of the large intestine was far advanced. We have done the only thing possible to save his life: we have cut the putrified section and joined the bowel together where the tissue was healthy. We believe he will survive.'

La Dusa knew that Mollini's convalescence would be long. She rented a house in a nearby street, so that she could come at any hour of the day or night to visit her love.

In the days following the operation, Mollini seemed, very slowly, to be getting well and La Dusa was full of praise for the surgeon who had saved his life. But then, on the fifth day, the wound became infected. Mollini's temperature soared and pain returned. For the first time, the nurses became attentive and La Dusa thought again of the beautiful hand pointing downwards to the morgue and became convinced that Mollini was going to die.

She had dreams of her lost wedding. In them, the forty-two swans Mollini had ordered were black. She made a decision. She would not let Mollini die before they were joined in marriage. She asked for the priest to be sent. He arrived with his candle and his holy water, thinking he was needed to administer the last rites. But no, La Dusa told him, she wanted him to marry them. The priest looked at Mollini and shook his head. He couldn't marry them if the groom was too ill to speak, he told her, and went away, giving La Dusa a strange and suspicious look.

She was in despair. She sat and watched her lover's life ebb.

But Mollini didn't die. His body's own magnificent healing powers surprised even the surgeon by fighting the infection till it was finally vanquished. He sat up. He began to eat, to laugh, to hold Verena's hand in a strong grip.

They returned to the Villa Mollini. The chapel was finished. Rain had come and the lake was brimming. In September, Verena Dusa and Antonio Mollini were married. The bride wore white satin and swans' feathers in her hair.

In the years that followed, all the original plans made by

27

Mollini and Pappavincente for the garden were imple-
mented. Every statue, every shrub, every rockery and
fountain was in place. 'All we can do now, Master,' said
Pappavincente, 'is to wait for everything to grow.' But
Mollini, whose fame and wealth had already grown to
giant proportions, began to conceive the idea of buying
land beyond the forest, of making pathways through the
forest in order to extend his garden to the other side of it.
He liked what had been achieved so far. He was especially
proud of the winding maze that led down to the lake, but
there were no surprises for him in the garden any more. As
he turned each corner, he knew exactly what he was going
to see.

The land on the other side of the wood was common
land, used by the villagers as pasture for their animals.
Pappavincente was told to go down to the village and
inform the farmers that ten hectares of pastureland were
going to be fenced off. He refused to go. He was ageing
and growing stubborn as he aged. 'Very well,' said
Mollini, 'I shall go myself.'

He didn't often visit the village now. He had long ago
stopped making his list of the names of the villagers'
children and he couldn't, in fact, remember the surnames
of many of the villagers themselves. He knew, however,
that the oldest man of the village, Emilio Verri, had
recently died. So Mollini decided to go straight to the
house of his widow, allegedly to offer his condolences.

Signora Verri was an old, old woman. 'I lost a husband,
and you, Signor Mollini, you lost your beloved wife,' she
said as the great man bent over her and put his hand on her
bony shoulders. Mollini straightened up. He couldn't
stand it when anyone mentioned Rosa's death. 'That was
long ago, Signora,' he said, 'and anyway, I have some
good news to cheer you up. My wife, Verena, is expecting
a child.'

The old crone lifted her face.

'A child, Signor Mollini?'

'Yes. In the spring.'

Signora Verri's eyes were wet. To her, a new child was
still a miracle of God.

'God bless the child, Sir.'

'Yes. He will be blessed, I'm sure. And I wanted to tell you something else. I am going to buy from the village – at a price that will keep you all in clover for many months – a little land, about twelve hectares north of my forest. And on this land, do you know what I'm going to make?'

'No, Signor.'

'A child's garden.'

'Ah. A child's garden?'

'Yes. It will be full of wonders. There will be peacocks and guinea fowl and rabbits and doves and goldfish and little houses in the trees and an aviary and a secret cave and hundreds of thousands of flowers.'

Signora Verri went to the door of her house and called her sons. There were three of them. Their handshakes were hard and their teeth yellowed from pipe tobacco. They demanded at once to know what price Mollini would pay for the land, explaining that a loss of twelve hectares would mean a reduction in livestock.

'A fair price,' said Mollini. 'What's more, I will buy all the livestock you have to slaughter and put the carcasses in my ice house till my son is born, and then there will be a huge feast and everyone in the village will be invited.'

He got away as quickly as he could. He looked back and saw the men of the village standing about in little groups, talking anxiously. But he wasn't worried. They'd get used to the idea of the loss of their pasture just as they'd got used to getting their water supply from containers and not from the river. They know, he told himself, that the only thing, apart from their children, which brings honour into their miserable lives is my fame. People of this calibre will sacrifice a lot to keep their dignity.

He was able to tell Pappavincente that the fencing of the land could begin straight away. 'No, Master,' said Pappavincente, 'the ground is much too hard. We shall have to wait till the frosts are over.'

Mollini agreed reluctantly. It was a very cold winter. Parts of the lake were frozen. Irritatingly, quite a few of the evergreens in the garden had died and the camellias were showing signs of winter damage. All of these would have to be torn out and replaced.

Mollini walked in the forest with his wife and showed her which ways the paths would go. They would zig-zag and cross each other, he explained. Then, little Pietro would be able to play games of tracking and hide-and-seek.

Although she tried not to show it, it saddened Verena that she was going to have to call her son Pietro. She liked the name Giuseppe, which was her father's name. But she was relieved to be pregnant at last. She was thirty-nine. Mollini had been nagging her for four years, ever since their first passionate year of love was over, to conceive. She'd tried very hard. She'd pampered herself with mounds of nutritious food. She'd even turned down an engagement to sing *Lucia di Lammermoor* in London, in order to follow Mollini to Vienna, so that he could make love to her at the right time of the month. She'd begun to fear that she would never conceive and she thought that if she didn't, it was possible that Mollini would leave her. My love is unquenchable, his is not, she told herself.

When her breasts began to swell and the time for her period had passed, she sent for the doctor. It was the same doctor who had given Mollini his enema and seen the slime in his bowel. He rolled up his sleeves. He inserted two icy fingers into Verena's vagina and pressed on her belly with the palm of the other hand. 'Well,' he said at last, as he disinfected his hands, 'your husband's wish has been granted.'

She decked herself in fussy, voluptuous gowns. Her bosom became gargantuan and she liked to show it off with lace frills and little cheeky ribbons. She didn't mind that she was getting ridiculously fat. She revelled in it. And Mollini too, from the moment he knew she was expecting his child, seemed to fall in love with her all over again. Even in public, he often couldn't refrain from fondling her breasts and whispering deliciously dirty suggestions in her ear. She giggled and screeched. She was delirious with happiness.

Several rooms in the Villa Mollini were being prepared for the baby. Nurses were interviewed and two engaged for the end of April. In March, the weather grew warmer. The fencing off of the twelve hectares was completed. Nine bullocks were slaughtered and stored in the ice house. In the forest, trees were felled to make way for the paths, wire for the aviary was ordered from Florence and a million bulbs came by cart from Holland.

Then, on the night of April 1st, a cold, relentless wind began to blow from the north. This wind terrified Verena. She liked Nature to be quiet. She put her head under her coverlet and encircled her unborn baby with her hands. An hour later, her waters broke.

The midwife came stumbling through the wind, holding her shawl round her chin. In the Villa Mollini, all the lamps were lit and the servants woken from sleep. Mollini stared at the midwife scuttling about with her towels and her basins and thought of all the births that had occurred in the village since he'd built his dam. Children were alive in the village who had never seen the river.

He went, feeling anxious, and sat on his own in his music room. Upstairs, Verena was behaving like a courageous rower, pushing with the tides. The seas were stormy. The pain tore at Verena's body and the wind tore at the garden, disturbing its order.

At dawn, the baby was born. It was a boy. It weighed less than two kilogrammes. Its first cry was feeble because, despite its magnificent parentage, its lungs were not properly formed. It gasped and gasped, like a little slithery eel, for air, and died within two hours.

Verena screamed till she was sick. The wind, blowing in the direction of the village, carried her screams to the ears of the villagers as the women made coffee and the men put on their working clothes.

It was strange. A few days after the baby died, Mollini sent for Pappavincente to tell him to redesign the child's garden, and then he changed his mind. Although there was

31

now no son to inhabit the garden, Mollini realised that he still wanted it made, exactly as he'd planned it.

'Master,' said Pappavincente, 'you will never bear to walk in it.'

'Then someone else will.'

'Who, Sir?'

'We shall see.'

Verena, huge in the bed, her breasts full of milk, announced: 'I never want to sing again. I'm going to cancel all my contracts.'

In May, Mollini left for Paris, where he was to sing Lensky in *Eugene Onegin*. Before leaving, he looked at his fat wife. She nourished herself, he decided, her own greedy flesh, not the baby's. She was still ridiculously gross and the baby, his poor little Pietro, was a tiny, sickly fish.

Verena didn't want Mollini to go to Paris. 'This world,' she said, 'this world we inhabit of roles and costumes and competition and money isn't worth a thing.' And she held Mollini so tightly to her that he felt himself suffocating. For the first time since he met her, he longed to be away from her, miles and miles away.

On the morning of his departure, Pappavincente came to see Mollini. He told him that wire for the aviary had arrived and asked him whether he should employ builders to start work on it. 'Of course,' said Mollini, 'of course.'

As the summer was coming, Mollini had decided to rent a house rather than an apartment in Paris. It wasn't far from the Bois de Boulogne. It had a pretty courtyard with a fountain.

In this house, a long way from Verena, he felt his sadness begin to ebb and his energy return. He gave a party on a warm June evening. A string quartet played Mozart. Sitting by his fountain, he saw bats circling over the city and remembered Rosa. He shuddered. He took the white wrist of his young co-star, Clara Buig, and held it to his lips. I will amuse myself, he decided, by making love to Clara.

La Buig was twenty-two. She was French. Paris

thought her enchanting. Her career was at its beginning. She wasn't known outside her country yet, but to be singing Tatiana to Mollini's Lensky would soon ensure her international status.

When Mollini's party was over, La Buig stayed behind. Mollini undressed her tenderly, as he would have undressed a child. She was slim and pale. 'Do you like gardens, Clara?' he asked.

Mollini was now forty-eight. Clara Buig was young enough to be his daughter. When he touched her, her eyes watched him gravely.

The next morning, he woke alone. He sent a servant with a note inviting Clara to lunch. But Mademoiselle Buig was not at home, she was working with her voice coach. Mollini went early to the Opéra. When La Buig arrived, she was wearing a pale lemon-coloured dress. She moved very gracefully, Mollini noted, like a dancer.

After the rehearsal, he invited her to supper. They would dine in the Bois after going for a stroll under the chestnut trees. But she refused. She was very tired, she said. To sing well, she needed a lot of rest.

Mollini went back to his house and sat by his fountain. He loved Paris. No other city satisfied the eye so agreeably. I shall stay here till autumn, he decided. It's so hot in Tuscany in the summer and here, it's cool. But he knew that if he stayed till autumn, Verena would arrive, with her trunks full of dresses and jewellery and her fan collection and her maids and her boxes of sweets. The thought of this arrival dismayed him. Hastily, he sat down and wrote to his wife. He informed her that there was a typhoid epidemic in Paris. 'I implore you, do not come near the city,' he wrote. 'For my sake, my love.'

And every time he saw Clara Buig, her sweet neck, her shy smile, her expressive hands, it was as if he was seeing a corner of his garden that he'd never noticed, never expected to be there, but which, given his care and his talents, would one day be the most beautiful place of all. As the days passed, he became more and more convinced that Clara Buig could not be absent from his future.

He waited. He had to wait patiently. His invitations to supper were, night after night, refused. 'Why?' he asked eventually. 'Why, Clara?'

She took his hand, noticing as she did so that several of his nails were bitten. 'The night of your party, I was so excited,' she said, 'so flattered. I just let myself go. I couldn't help it.'

'And was that wrong, my adorable Clara?'

'Oh yes. But I won't let it happen again.'

So, only on stage did she look at him adoringly. Outside the Opéra, she refused ever to be alone with him.

Verena wrote to him almost every day. Her fortieth birthday was approaching. She was depressed. She begged Mollini to let her know the moment the typhoid epidemic was over so that she could come to Paris and be with him. She told him that the loss of their child had only deepened her love for him.

What she didn't say in her letters, because at first she didn't notice it, was that since the second week of April no rain had fallen and that the level of the lake was going down fast as the villagers pumped out more and more water for their potato crop, for their vines, for their thirsty animals.

Pappavincente was worried about all the new shrubs he'd planted in the child's garden. Water containers were driven through the new paths in the forest. He and the other gardeners spent two hours every evening going round with watering cans.

One evening, Pappavincente took a walk up the valley. He saw that the river was dangerously low and he remembered with dread the terrible drought of 1856, when all the villages along the valley began desperately trying to sink new wells and when his grandmother had wondered aloud whether Pappavincente's existence wasn't to blame for all the anxiety and suffering.

As he walked back towards the lake, he saw La Dusa standing by it, holding a parasol. He bowed to her. She was dressed in grey satin with a high lace collar and, with her feet tucked into red shoes, Pappavincente thought she looked like a fat pigeon. Her once beautiful eyes were now just two dark pleats in the flesh of her face.

'I'm so sorry, Signora,' said Pappavincente, 'about the baby . . .'

'Yes,' said La Dusa and waddled away up the path to the forest, carrying her weight, as she carried her sorrow, awkwardly.

The forest was cool. A hundred times, Verena had rehearsed in her mind the day when she would push the ornate baby carriage under the magnificent fans of oak and beech and watch the dappling of sunlight on her son, Giuseppe. Now, she was there alone. And it was her birthday. She stopped and folded her parasol and examined her hands for signs of age. Mollini's wedding ring was wedged so tightly onto her finger, she was unable, these days, to take it off. 'Look at these fat hands!' she said aloud and recalled with a strange kind of fascination the beautifully drawn thin hand pointing downwards to the hospital morgue.

She'd intended to visit the child's garden. Mollini had refused to discuss with her his decision to carry on with the project and the thought of this garden being designed and planted for someone who would never see it filled her with sadness. She found, as she neared it and caught sight of the half-completed aviary that she really didn't want to go there, and anyway she was out of breath.

She returned to the house. On the first terrace she noticed that the drains were stinking again. The smell was disgusting, but she lingered near it for a moment. It reminded her of happier times.

On the opening night of *Eugene Onegin*, La Dusa arrived, uninvited, in Paris.

Mollini's house was filled with servants preparing for a party. Lanterns had been lit all round the courtyard and tables set up near the fountain.

Mollini wasn't there. La Dusa dressed herself in a white gown and put feathers in her hair. She didn't go to the Opéra, but sat in the cool garden sipping champagne and questioning the servants about the typhoid epidemic. 'What typhoid epidemic?' they inquired politely.

When Mollini returned, Clara Buig was with him, holding on to his arm. La Dusa looked at them. Mollini had grown a beard, put on weight. He looked like an English king. When he saw his wife, he bowed – just as Pappavincente had bowed to her beside the lake – and led Clara Buig forward and introduced her formally. La Dusa didn't get up. She ignored Clara's outstretched hand, but reached up and pulled Mollini towards her, so that he stumbled and fell into her lap. She bit his ear. 'If you lie to me again, Antonio, I shall kill you,' she said.

Two weeks later, they returned together to the Villa Mollini. On the journey, Mollini feigned illness, a return of the pain in his bowel. And it was true, he was suffering. He was now madly, dementedly, obsessively in love with Clara Buig. He couldn't look at his wife, let alone touch her. All he could remember was the one beautiful night when Clara had let him love her, a night he had so carefully planned to repeat by giving a party in her honour.

He couldn't close his eyes without dreaming of Clara. Thoughts of her never left his mind. By the time he arrived at the Villa, he felt so troubled he had to sit down and write to her straight away and in the letter he found that he was telling her that he loved her more than he'd ever loved anyone, that his love for La Dusa had been pale in comparison. *Pale*? As he wrote this word, he couldn't help remembering certain nights, certain delectable afternoons he'd spent with Verena, but of course these had been long ago and she'd been beautiful then. And things pass, he said to himself. We move. The horizon changes. We turn a corner and a new sight greets us. This is how it has to be.

And to reassure himself, he went out into the garden. He was shocked at what he saw. The earth was parched. The smell near the house was terrible. Everywhere, as he strolled from path to path, from terrace to terrace, there were gaps in the borders and beds where plants had withered. The fountains had been turned off. The water in the fountain pools was bright green and foul-smelling. Mollini stood still and stared up at the sky. It was a deep, relentless blue. The sun on his face was fierce and all he could hear and feel was the buzzing and shimmering of the heat.

At that moment, he remembered the nine bullock carcasses. His stomach turned. Sorrow for his little dead child compounded his sickness. He sat down on a stone seat and put his head in his hands. The salt sweat from his brow stung his eyes.

He prayed the nausea would pass. It seemed like the nausea of death, when the appetite for the world drains, leaving the mind filled with loathing.

To soothe himself, he thought of his music. 'Mollini's voice is not simply a voice,' a Paris critic had declared, 'it is an instrument. I have never before heard such an astonishing sound come out of a man.' And the sickness did, after a while, begin to pass. So Mollini stood up. Instead of returning to the house – to Verena's tears and entreaties which only repelled him and were utterly in vain – he walked on down to the lake. It was no longer blue, but brownish and full of silt. He skirted it and went up into the forest. Here, it was cool. In the shade of the big trees, nettles and sweet briars were green.

He followed one of the winding paths. He began to feel better. If only, he thought, I could stroll here with Clara, with her little hand tucked into my arm.

As he neared the child's garden, he feared that all the new bushes and hedges planted in the spring would have died, but the moment he left the forest and came out again into the sunlight, he saw that everything here was living and healthy, that already roses were climbing up the trellises and that purple and white clematis were growing strongly up the sides of the aviary.

Mollini smiled. It was a smile of gratitude and a smile of hope renewed. As he looked at the faithful work of Pappavincente and the other gardeners, he knew why he had made them go on with the child's garden: he would give it to Clara.

In August, Mollini told Pappavincente that water to the village would have to be rationed. The ration was so meagre and insufficient that the young men led nightly raiding parties to the lake, carrying buckets and churns, but the water itself was becoming soupy and brackish and the villagers and their animals developed intestinal illnesses.

Then, the widow Verri died. Mollini attended the funeral. He sensed, for the first time, that his presence among the villagers no longer filled them with pride. As he held out his hand for them to shake, they let their fingers touch his, but wouldn't hold his hand in a firm grip. To cheer them up and win back their reverence, he invited them to come and see the child's garden and to drink wine with him on the site of the summer house he was planning to build there.

So they came one morning and stood about awkwardly. The garden was beautiful, lush and healthy. They touched the flowers. The scent of them was extraordinary. They'd forgotten how superb the world could seem. They drank the dry white wine, bottle after bottle, and staggered home in mid-afternoon to dream muddled dreams. Before they left, Mollini had embraced the men and kissed the women on the lips. 'I made them happy,' he told Verena.

Verena didn't move out of her room these days. She sat up in her bed and fed her sorrow with sweet wine and chocolate. Her feet began to swell and the doctor was called. Verena burst into tears. 'I know what would cure me,' she sobbed, 'if Antonio would only take me in his arms . . .' The doctor went away, disgusted.

'My wife is suffering,' Mollini wrote to Clara, 'and I cannot help but feel sorry for her. But her suffering is nothing to my own: I'm in love with a woman I cannot marry.'

In September, Mollini left for Vienna. He was to take on his most demanding and difficult role, in Verdi's *Otello*. He had signed the contract on one condition, that the part of Desdemona be given to Clara Buig. And in Vienna at last Clara became Mollini's mistress. She had been so moved, she said, by his letters, she knew she could no longer resist.

He was in heaven. La Buig wasn't a sensual woman like La Dusa. There were moments, even, when her grave face beneath his reminded Mollini of Rosa's face, long, long ago. 'You give our love nobility and dignity,' he told Clara, 'you turn the past into the future.'

He was determined, now, that there would be a future with Clara. He wrote to Pappavincente with new designs for the summer house. It would no longer be a summer house: it would have a sumptuous bedroom and bathroom and fires in all the rooms. It would be Clara's residence.

As rumours of the love affair of Antonio Mollini and the 23-year-old Clara Buig spread in whispers round the tea-rooms and the musical salons of Vienna, it began at last to rain in Tuscany. It rained for seventeen days and nights. The villagers came out of their hovels and stuck their tongues out and let the sweet rain trickle down their throats. Verena got out of bed, threw a shawl round her shoulders and walked out in the downpour to the lake side. The water had risen by several feet. Verena walked into the water, wearing her pink satin slippers. The slippers stuck in the mud, so she waded on without them, feeling her petticoats and her skirt become heavy.

She lay on her back. She expected to sink straight away, but her large body was buoyant and she found that she was floating. She stared at the grey sky and thought how astonishingly full of colour her life had been. It took her three hours to die. On the brink of death, it seemed to La Dusa that the grey cloud moved away and that the hot sun was shining on her round face. And for a second, she imagined the autumn to come and the wonderful vibrant reds and umbers of the leaves.

By the time the winter came, Clara's house was finished. Mollini, however, didn't bother to have the fires lit.

'Clara will live with me in the Villa Mollini,' he told

Pappavincente, so the shutters were closed and the place locked.

When Clara Buig at last arrived at the Villa Mollini, however, and was led by a maid to the very room La Dusa had occupied, she refused to sleep there. The house, in fact, gave her the creeps, she said. She couldn't possibly spend a night in it.

Mollini wrapped her in her velvet coat and walked with her, arm in arm, through the garden, round the lake and up into the forest. The great trees were silent. Winter had begun to bite early this year.

The pleasure Mollini took from seeing Clara's little gloved hand on his arm was acute, too precious and fleeting to mention. They walked on in silence, descending at last down the intricate paths of the child's garden to Clara's house. Golden pheasants in the aviary squawked and pecked at the wire as they passed.

Mollini opened the shutters of the house and got on his knees and lit a fire in one of the grates.

Clara walked on her own from room to room and then went outside again and walked all round the house. It was nicely set in the child's garden, surrounded by stone terraces and ornate balustrading and small cypresses. At the back of it, however, about forty yards away, Clara could see an ugly post-and-rails fence and beyond this a boring slope of empty pastureland.

'What is that?' she asked Mollini.

Mollini had followed her outside and now looked to where she was pointing.

'Common land,' said Mollini. 'The village people use it to graze their cattle.'

La Buig sniffed. Then she turned her stern child's face towards Mollini and said: 'You know what I would like to see there instead of that?'

'No, my love.'

'An English lawn. This whole garden is nothing but steps and piazzas and gazebos and mazes and borders and beds. If I'm going to live here, I really want a lawn.'

Mollini sent for Pappavincente. One of his sons arrived

40

instead and told him that Pappavincente was ill and couldn't come.

Mollini went at once to the village, not to tell the people that he was going to take away the rest of their pasture for Clara's lawn, but to see the old man and take him some of the strong red wine he knew he liked to drink.

'We believe he's dying,' said Signora Pappavincente. She was holding a rag to her nose, and when Mollini went into the room where Pappavincente lay, it seemed to him that the odour of death was indeed very strong.

'Listen, old friend,' he whispered to Pappavincente, 'remember all that you've achieved here. Dwell on that. Feel proud of it. You've made the most beautiful garden in Tuscany, perhaps the most beautiful garden in all Italy. And it's not finished yet. It lives on. It changes and grows. It will last for ever.'

Pappavincente's head rolled on the pillow and he turned his staring, angry eyes on Mollini. 'I have sinned, Master,' he said.

He died that night. Mollini wanted him buried in the garden, but the old man's family were stubborn and wouldn't allow it.

Mollini explained to Clara that the whole village would be in mourning for a while and that it would be impossible, just at the moment, to mention the land he was going to take for her lawn.

'I understand,' said Clara, 'but you will tell them in the spring?'

'Yes. In the spring.'

'Because I want to push my baby's bassinet on the lawn. Like an English duchess. You see?'

'Your baby's bassinet, Clara?'

'Yes, Antonio. I'm going to have your child.'

Mollini took Clara's serious little face in his hands and covered it with kisses. Three weeks later, he married her. Once again, the cream of the opera world was invited to the Villa Mollini. Among the cream was an extra-ordinarily beautiful English soprano called Marion Shepherd. Marion Shepherd told Mollini that she thought his garden was as unbelievable as his voice and smiled such a dazzling smile that Mollini was forced to reach out and caress her mouth with his finger.

On the wedding night, Clara Buig was very restless. The baby inside her, little Pietro, as Mollini called him, kept kicking her and her head seemed to be full of strange visions and fears.

The dawn was icy cold, but as soon as the sky was light, Clara got up and dressed herself and went out into the garden. She didn't wake Mollini. He lay snoring on his back with his legs apart.

She walked towards the Villa Mollini itself, which seemed to beckon her. On the way, she came across an old stone well with delicate arching ironwork that she'd never noticed before. I expect it's just ornamental, she thought, like everything else in this garden. But she was curious about it, so she walked to the edge of it and peered in. Much to her surprise, she found that she was looking down into darkness.

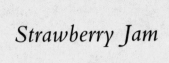

Strawberry Jam

WHEN I WAS fourteen, in 1957, my mother died. We buried her in the village graveyard and I wore new black shoes with high heels at her funeral. Sudden loss and the pinch of fashionable shoes were then and ever afterwards connected in my mind. I still feel my own mortality most acutely in my feet.

It was winter. My father studied recipes for hot puddings. 'Staying alive means keeping warm,' he said. Suet and sponge were it, our existence. Yet I was growing, getting tall and thin, and these limbs of mine were as cold as marble. I put the high-heeled shoes away, wrapped up in tissue paper. When I remembered my mother, I thought about my own vanity and wondered when my life would begin. Passion, I believed, might warm me up. Folded inside one of my bedsocks was a photograph of Alan Ladd.

As the spring came and the evenings got lighter, I spent a lot of time looking out of my window, as if trying to see in the familiar landscape of our neighbours' garden the arrival of the future. This garden, separated from ours by only a picket fence, was never ever dug, pruned or tended in any way and in summer puffs of seed streamed off into the wind from its thistles and willow-herb and tall grasses, sowing themselves in our lawn and in my mother's rockery. She had been a polite and timid person. Only once had she plucked up her courage and knocked on our neighbours' back door and announced with great grief in

45

her voice: 'Your weeds are making my task very difficult, Mr Zimmerli.' Walter Zimmerli had come out and stared at his wilderness, sizing it up like a man at a heifer auction.

'The weeds?'

'Yes. They re-seed themselves all over the place.'

'And the solution?'

'Well, if you could root them out . . .'

'But look how splendid is the pink colour!'

'I know . . .'

'We like this: nature not disturbed. This is important to Jani, I'm afraid.'

The only trees in the Zimmerlis' garden were fruit trees: an old and graceful Victoria Plum, a crab apple and some lichen-covered Bramleys. Every Christmas, Walter Zimmerli set up a ladder and gathered the mistletoe that sprouted near the tops of the Bramleys. In summer, out came the ladder again and the crab apples and plums were picked, but most of the Bramleys left to the wasps and the autumn gales. We didn't know why at first, till Jani Zimmerli came round with a jar of crab apple jelly for us. My mother tried to thank her. 'It is not thanks,' said Jani, 'Walter and I, we love jam.'

So in April I watched the blossom creeping out on the Zimmerlis' trees and spots creeping out on my face. The sweet puddings streamed in my blood. My father began to learn the recipes by heart.

Then, Mrs Lund arrived.

I saw her first from my window. Walter and Jani Zimmerli came out into their orchard. It was dusk. Mrs Lund followed them like a little shadow. The three stood together quietly and stared at the trees. Mrs Lund set down the suitcase she was carrying and Walter turned to her and said something in German. Mrs Lund nodded and Jani nodded and then they picked up the suitcase and went back inside the house. At supper, I told my father: 'The Zimmerlis have got a friend staying.'

'Are you sure?'

'Yes. I saw her. She's quite old.'

My father put down his knife and fork on a plate of

dumplings and gravy he couldn't eat. 'I suppose you'll be keeping watch,' he said.

Watching the Zimmerlis had been an occupation of mine since the first summer of their arrival, but I used to watch the front of their house – from a window seat in our sitting room. I would wrap my face in the lace curtains and stare out at them. 'Holly!' my mother would snap. 'Leave them alone!' But I couldn't leave them alone because I was fascinated by what they were doing. Outside their door, on the grass verge, they'd set up a table, shaded on hot days by a large faded umbrella, and here they sat – sometimes both of them, sometimes Jani alone – hour after hour, waiting for people to pass. They were trying to sell jam. The jam was delicious – we were among the few who knew this – and Jani had made pretty gingham covers for the array of pots. But two things struck me as strange. First of all, our houses are on a narrow, out-of-the-way road down which almost no one travels, so that Jani and Walter could sit at their little stall for an entire afternoon without selling one single jar of jam. Secondly, whenever a car *did* stop, the Zimmerlis never seemed to be content with the small commercial transaction, but began to treat the customers like old friends, talking and laughing and invariably trying to persuade them to go into their house for a glass of sherry.

My mother didn't approve of my spying on the Zimmerlis. When I told her they invited strangers in, she didn't believe me. 'The Zimmerlis wouldn't do that,' she said, 'they keep themselves to themselves.' She died disbelieving me. She'd never heard them pleading with strangers, 'Just to keep a little company,' but I had. And I also knew something else: the jam customers were the *only* people who ever went into that house. No real friends ever arrived. We, their closest neighbours, were never invited past the kitchen door. They gave us jam. They said good evening from their perch up the ladders. But that was all. No car except theirs ever stood in the drive. Even at Christmas their house was silent and the door closed. No light ever went on in the guest room. It was as if they had

47

no past and courted no future, only this fleeting present – a few coins in the money tin and the company of strangers.

Now, this elderly woman had arrived. For the first time ever, a light went on in the Zimmerlis' spare room and I saw Jani at the window, drawing the curtains. I imagined this shadowy person, covered with the fat Austrian feather quilt, her possessions folded and put away. I imagined Jani and Walter next door to her, talking in whispers.

And then I learned her name. I was in our garden, putting new alpines in my mother's rockery. I looked up and saw someone standing at the picket fence and it was her. I smiled.

'Very good weather,' she said.

'Yes. The winter's over, probably.'

'I think you must be Holly?'

'Yes.'

'Well. Jani and Walter have spoken of you.'

'Have they?'

'Oh yes.'

I stood up. I thought about my face wrapped in the lace curtains, a gross, gawping bride. Since my mother's death, I suffered very often from shame.

'My name is Mrs Lund,' said the woman.

'How do you do?' I said.

The weather people told us a hot summer was coming. The weeds in the Zimmerlis' patch were growing green again through last year's fallen mass. I waited for the Zimmerlis to set up the jam stall, but it didn't appear. They had company now, they had Mrs Lund. I imagined them drinking sherry with her and talking about Viennese teashops full of delicate confectionery – apricot tartlets, apple flan, damson shortcake. She was their past, come to sweeten them, and for a time I envied them, because I knew my own past – our warm, comfortable life with my mother – could only come back as a cold memory. But after a few weeks of Mrs Lund's visit, I began to notice a change in the Zimmerlis: they were losing weight.

I had never known how old they were. Walter seemed older (fatter, with wilder greying hair) than my father, who was forty-three, and Jani seemed younger (more buxom, dimpled and healthy) than my mother, who had been forty-one. Certainly, I'd always thought of them as large, not bony and big as I was, but wide and squashy as only people nearing middle age become. But now they seemed reduced. Walter's belly was smaller; Jani's arms, hanging up her napkins and her tablecloths, were thinner. Even Walter's laugh, not often heard these days, seemed altered, no longer the laugh of a heavy man.

The diminution of the Zimmerlis struck me as odd. Then, one night very late (I'd taken Alan Ladd out of my bedsock and was smoothing him out on my dressing table) I heard Jani weeping. I turned my light off and went to the window. Jani was sitting on her terrace and her face was buried in her lap. After a while, Walter came out and knelt down beside her and leant his head against her shoulder. He spoke to her very softly and this was the first time that I ever thought of the German language as a comforting thing. But I also had a strong feeling – confirmed by my own sleeplessness – that something important was about to happen. And it did happen. That same night, Mrs Lund disappeared.

I woke very late the next morning. It was Saturday. An unfamiliar *chock*, *chock* sound had woken me. When I looked out, I saw what it was: Walter Zimmerli was digging his garden! I called my father and we watched him together. A large patch of weeds had already been cleared and Walter's back was soaked with sweat. He worked on without stopping, thrusting the spade into the earth, levering with his foot, smashing the clods as he turned them over.

'Why?' I whispered.

''Bout time, anyway,' said my father.

'Yes, but why? Why now?'

'Dunno, Holly. People are often a mystery. You'll find that out.'

My father went downstairs as I stayed at the window. Then my father returned with hot muffins and milky coffee on a tray. He said I needed spoiling. Grief, he said, is very tiring. He made me get back into bed to eat the breakfast. Then I dozed. I *was* tired. And I had a dream that Walter Zimmerli had killed Mrs Lund, smashed her on the back of the neck with a marble rolling pin, and buried her in the garden. That was why – yes, of course, that was why – Jani had wept. They had murdered Mrs Lund.

Then it was mid-day and I was at the window again. On and on Walter worked, with the spring sunshine hot on his neck. Nearly half of his garden had been cleared when I heard Jani call him in. He left his spade sticking into the earth.

His subterfuge isn't bad, I thought. If he'd cleared only a very small patch, a patch only three or four times larger, say, than the spot where Mrs Lund is buried, this might have appeared odd. As it is, he pretends he's weeding his whole garden, getting rid of the willow-herb at last, answering his neighbours' complaints. But he hasn't fooled me! I saw Mrs Lund die in my dream. I saw Walter go out and begin to dig in the dead of morning. I saw Jani trying to help him, pulling with all her might at the grasses. Then I saw them go inside and wrap Mrs Lund's body in a faded rug and stagger out, one holding her shoulders, one her feet, and lay her in a shallow trough that was only just deep enough to hide her. They smashed her in. Hurriedly, Walter piled the earth on top of her and began – even though he was tired by this time and aching with fear – to turn the soil around and beyond the grave. And this is when I began to hear it, the *chock*, *chock* of his terrible digging . . .

I don't remember what we did that weekend. I know my father took me out somewhere, to see my cousins perhaps, who lived in a big house by a river. All I know is that Walter Zimmerli worked on and on, almost without pausing until, by dusk on Sunday, no trace of the grass or thistle or willow-herb remained and the earth was raked flat like a seed bed and in the twilight Jani made a bonfire of the weeds and I heard the Zimmerlis laughing.

During the next week, they began to plant. On their back porch were piles of wooden boxes stacked up. Each box contained twenty or thirty straggly plants and they set them in rows measured out with string about three feet apart. And I knew what they were: they were straw-berries. I wanted to say to my father, 'They're planting strawberries on Mrs Lund!' But I didn't. I just stood on our side of the picket fence and stared at the Zimmerlis crouched down and at Jani's skirt in the mud, and then I offered to help. They stood up and smiled at me. 'Ah,' said Walter, 'very fortunate, eh Jani? Holly can be in charge of the straw.'

As I worked, moving down the lines very slowly with the sacks of straw, I tried to test the feel of the earth under my boots. I knew where the body was – roughly – but the soil in the right hand corner of the garden was as flat and even as the rest. They did a good job, I thought. No one will ever know. *Except me.* Unless, of course, someone comes over from Vienna and they start to search. And I imagined how it would be then: they would find traces of Mrs Lund's visit in the house – tweed skirts, shoes of Swiss leather, a tortoiseshell hairbrush bundled out of sight in a wardrobe – and then of course they would begin to dig . . .

We finished planting the strawberries the following weekend. My father said I looked pink from all the fresh air and work, and I did find that my skinny hands and feet had been warmed up. Alan Ladd in my bedsock felt snug. And then the strangest, most unexpected thing happened: Walter Zimmerli gave me a key to his house. 'We have to go away, Holly,' he said. 'We have to go back to Vienna to sort out some papers and things and we would be so grateful if you might water our many house plants.'

'Yes,' said Jani, 'we would be grateful. But we ask you not to touch anything, any precious things, and let no one else come in. We trust you to be this little caretaker.'

I looked at the Zimmerlis: two solemn faces; two bodies, once weighty, growing thin with anxiety and guilt. 'Of course,' I said. 'I'd be happy to take care of your plants. And if the weather's very dry, I'll put our sprinkler on the strawberries.'

It was May. For my birthday, my father bought me a blue and white polka–dot skirt and a white webbing belt. He said I was getting to look like Debbie Reynolds. 'My hair's thin,' I said, 'perhaps it's our diet.' So he started to learn a new set of recipes, casseroles and hotpots and fruit fools, and we began to flourish.

Crime detection, wrote the Chief Constable of the Suffolk Police in our church news sheet, *requires faith, hope, intelligence and also physical courage*. I cut these words out and hid them in a shell box my mother had given me. The Zimmerlis left very early one morning and all the blinds and shutters in the house were closed.

'I have a feeling,' I said to my father, 'that they'll never come back.'

'Why do you think that?'

'I don't know,' I said dreamily, 'I have these peculiar thoughts.'

I made myself wait one week before going into the Zimmerlis' house. I ate well and went for long rides on my bicycle to make myself strong. Then I chose a Sunday morning. My father had gone to the pub. I took a watering-can and the door key and a wire coat-hanger. When I opened the Zimmerlis' back door, all I could see was darkness.

I was looking for two things: the murder weapon and the locked wardrobe. I flicked a light switch in the hall, but no light came on. The electricity had been turned off. I made my way in the dark to the kitchen. I set down the watering-can. Slowly, I tipped the slats of the Venetian blinds and sunlight fell in stripes onto the scrubbed table and an ornate dresser painted red and green. I opened every drawer and found all kinds of utensil – whisks and strainers, graters and slicers and scoops – but no rolling pin. *The murder weapon*, said the voice of the Chief Constable, *is seldom easily found. However, it is sometimes possible to infer guilt precisely from the* absence *of the instrument of death from its accustomed place.*

I stood and looked at the room where Jani Zimmerli had made her cauldrons of jam. Was it possible that this Austrian woman with her sweet tooth never made pastry? Never made flans or strudel or pies? I didn't think so. I imagined Walter and Jani – at least until they began to get thin – living on this kind of food, and yet nowhere in the kitchen could I find a rolling pin.

There were some fleshy plants on the window sill. I ran water into my can and doused them, pondering what to do next. No doubt my search for the rolling pin was futile. It lay, I imagined, in the mud of the river that flowed past my cousins' house. When the summer holidays came, I would announce a diving competition. Meanwhile, I had to find the locked wardrobe.

I made my way upstairs, carrying the wire hanger. I knew which side of the house the guest room was on, but I decided, first, to go into the Zimmerlis' own bedroom. Drawing the heavy curtains, I noticed that the room had a strange smell. The odour in this one room was warm and spicy, as if Jani and Walter had been in it only moments before. I looked at the bed, covered with a heavy, intricate patchwork quilt and at Jani's little dressing-table mirror draped with scarves and amber beads and a sudden, unexpected feeling of sadness came to me. It was obvious – so obvious! – that Jani and Walter had been happy here, in this room, in this house, but now, because of what they had done, their happiness was over and they would never be able to come back here. Change had come. To them. To me. Mrs Lund lay under the strawberries; my mother lay under the churchyard turf. One part of my life was gone.

I sat down on the Zimmerlis' bed. I didn't cry. I made myself think about Alan Ladd and French kissing and the future. I promised myself I would take my black high heels out of the tissue paper and try them on.

I got up and smoothed the quilt and walked, upright and purposeful, to the room where Mrs Lund had slept. I lifted the blind and looked around. There were two beds in the room, both narrow. Between them was an old washstand with a flowery jug and bowl. On the wood floor was a faded rug resembling almost perfectly the rug I'd seen in my dream. In the corner of the room, behind the door, was a mahogany wardrobe. This was so exactly like the wardrobe I'd imagined (mirror glass on the front, ornate classical carvings along the top) that I caught my breath and now hardly dared to move towards it. I looked down at the wire coat-hanger in my hand. In stories, people opened doors with coat-hangers, but would I be able to do it? I stepped forward. Only then did I notice that the key of the wardrobe was there in the lock.

Over the years, I've thought about it very many times, that moment of opening the wardrobe in Mrs Lund's room. I see myself exactly as I was then, reflected in the mirror, wearing my blue polka-dot skirt, my face solemn but full of expectation, on the brink of a momentous discovery. And then I see the inside of the wardrobe, not, as I had imagined, filled with Mrs Lund's possessions, but completely empty except for one small object, a black leatherbound notebook. These things made a kind of tableau, like a snapshot. I caught it then and I have it still in my mind, a split second of the future, waiting.

I picked up the notebook, sat down on one of the beds and opened it. On the first page, in fine italic handwriting were the words: *Tagebuch von J.B. Zimmerli* – the diary of J.B. Zimmerli. Above the first entry were written the date and place: *Wien, November 1937*. I turned the pages, understanding hardly a word of the careful handwriting, but noting dates and places. The entries ceased, with several blank pages remaining, in March 1938. As I came to the final entry, something fell out of the notebook onto the floor. I picked it up. It was a photograph of two children, a boy and a girl, aged perhaps ten and eight respectively. It was summer in the picture. The two children squinted into bright light. Behind them was the glimpse of a lake.

That night, I tried to sort it all out in my head. I'd found nothing in the Zimmerlis' house, apart from the absence of the rolling pin, that proved them guilty of Mrs Lund's murder. No possessions stowed away, no sign of her suitcase. I'd gone into every room. I'd tried to think clearly, like a proper detective, aware that clues are not always hidden, but sometimes in plain view, but the longer I searched, the more I began to doubt my first conclusion. It was possible, after all, that Mrs Lund had left very late on the night that I saw Jani crying. A taxi could have come for her, or Walter could have driven her to the station. Perhaps, even, she had left *before* Jani's weeping and it was precisely because Mrs Lund had left that Jani was so upset? And what about the digging? Well, here too, there were logical explanations: Walter's neighbours, including my mother, had been nagging him to do something about his weeds for long enough. Perhaps Mrs Lund, too, had ticked him off and even given him the idea of planting the strawberries.

I decided I would let the whole matter rest for a while. Already my brain felt tired with it and I was beginning to feel glad that I didn't work for the Suffolk Constabulary. I would go in from time to time and water the house plants and I would make sure the strawberries didn't die. And I would wait. In time, I thought, I will probably understand.

The only thing I'd taken from the house was the photograph of the children. I looked at it for a long time and the longer I looked, the more I became convinced that these were the children of Walter and Jani. Because it had always seemed strange to me that the Zimmerlis, who appeared so contented with each other, hadn't got their own family. Had something terrible happened to these children? Was it for them that Jani cried? Were the strangers, clutching their pots of jam, the only people to be told of the tragedy? Was this their *function*, to be silent, anonymous listeners? My father often said he found it easier to talk about my mother's death to strangers than to his friends. One day, he said, he told the lift-man at his office and the lift-man had been very nice to him. If this was true for my father, perhaps it was true for Walter and Jani?

As the days passed, I found I was getting very fond of the photograph. I could imagine the scenery behind the children: the huge lake, a hazy shore line, incredible mountains with snow on their peaks. It calmed me to think of a foreign place – as if part of the future might take place in it. I hid the photograph in my other bedsock, but the nights were warmer now, so the socks and the pictures lay folded under my pillow.

As the weathermen had predicted, that summer of 1957 was very hot. Through the first two weeks of June, my father and I watered the Zimmerlis' strawberries and by the third week the strawberries were ripe. There was no sign of Walter and Jani and birds had already begun to peck at the fruit. We stood by our fence and surveyed the crop.

'Terrible waste,' said my father.

'Let's pick them,' I said, 'and make jam.'

We bought a preserving pan. In our larder, we found dozens of jam jars, brown with dust, saved by my mother for this day she would never see. On the evening the jam was labelled and put back into the larder – thirteen pounds of it in twenty-one jars – Walter and Jani returned. We saw them kneeling down in the strawberry beds and lifting the leaves to search for the fruit. I called from my upstairs window: 'Don't worry! It's all safe!' And when I took the jam round to them the next day, their gratitude seemed to overflow, as if I'd brought them something of great value.

'So *kind*, Walter, isn't it?' said Jani, picking up one of the pots. 'So much work and kindness.'

'Indeed,' said Walter, 'indeed this is most thoughtful.'

'You could sell it on the road,' I suggested.

'Yes,' said Jani, 'but you must have all the money. Holly must have the profit.'

'Yes,' said Walter, 'and next year too. The plants will grow a little larger and we shall have a better crop.'

'It's kind of you,' I said, 'but you don't have to give me any money.'

'But we want to do this,' said Jani, 'maybe you can buy a polka blouse to match your skirt.'

I returned the house key to them. As I went to the door, Jani came with me and put her arm, which was still much thinner than it had once been, round my shoulders. 'Like you,' she said, 'we have had some sad times. We lost Walter's mother.'

'She died?'

'Yes. In one way so sad, yet in one way happy. Walter's father was killed by the Nazis in 1938 and, since this time, his mother was all these years in an institution, not know-ing really what the days were, but thinking the time is before the war and she is a girl again, like you. In her last days, she says to the nurse, do my breasts grow?'

'I'm very sorry,' I said.

'Yes,' said Jani, 'sorrow for all. But that is why we put in the strawberries: *Mutti's* favorite fruit.'

I pieced it together then. Mrs Lund – an old friend of the family? – had been a courier. She'd brought not only the news of the death of Walter's mother, but had come to hand over the few possessions of the dead woman, the most important of which was the diary belonging to her husband, J.B. Zimmerli. It was for Walter's mother that Jani had wept, and it was their mourning that had made them thin. There was no body in the garden. The only bit of the mystery I couldn't solve was the identity of the children and I thought now that I never would.

I knew I had to find a way to return the photograph to the wardrobe in Mrs Lund's room, and I had made a plan. I would offer to help the Zimmerlis with their jam stall. On a hot afternoon, I would ask them if I could go into the kitchen for a glass of water – a request they couldn't refuse. Then, quickly and silently, I would go upstairs and return the photograph to the black notebook.

But I wanted to have one last look at it. I went up to my room and reached under my pillow to pull out my bed-socks, but they weren't there. With feelings of guilt and dread, I began to search my cupboards and drawers. Alan Ladd I could replace, but those children by the lake, that picture was perhaps all that remained of them. I looked out at the Zimmerlis' house. They'd trusted me, called me their 'caretaker' and I'd betrayed them.

And then I saw my bedsocks. They were hanging on the washing line. I ran down to the garden, past my father who was sitting in the sun. I unpegged the socks, which were still damp. 'Need them,' I said to my father and fled back up to my room.

I put my hand into each of them in turn. Alan Ladd, made of inferior paper, was scrunched into a ball no bigger than a marble. I threw him into my waste paper basket. But the photograph of the children had survived. It was only slightly creased and not faded at all.

I held it against my face, smoothing it out. And then I noticed that there *was* something different about it. Before the washing, the photograph had been backed with thick, black paper, as if it had been stuck into an album and cut out with part of the album page still glued to it. Now, the black layer of paper wasn't there. I turned the photograph over. In the bottom right hand corner of it, a faded caption was still just decipherable: Dated 1926, it read: *Walter und Jani an der See.* And I understood.

For four years, I kept the Zimmerlis' secret. In precisely the way I had planned, I returned the photograph to the notebook and of course Jani and Walter never mentioned either the diary or the picture to me. I grew fond of them and they seemed to become fond of me, yet on certain days, for no reason at all, they would behave very coldly towards me, as if they were saying to me, 'Don't come too close. Friendship is too knowing. We prefer still, as always, to talk to the strangers, who will never find out anything and who will never come back.'

And so, hurt one day by a rebuff of Jani's – 'Holly, go home now. You talk too much, always of boyfriends, always of your future. It's boring, you know.' – I decided to tell my father. We were sitting together in the kitchen. It was 1961. My father had encouraged his thinning hair to grow long over his ears. I took a sip of the white wine we were drinking and looked at my loving, would-be hippy dad and said solemnly: 'Walter and Jani Zimmerli are brother and sister.'

He smiled and nodded. 'Don't tell the vicar,' he said.

The morning I left home for my first term at university, I knocked on the Zimmerlis' back door to say goodbye. Jani opened it, her hands and arms covered in flour. 'I'm making pastry,' she said, 'come in.'

We went into her kitchen. I put the kettle on and watched her work. Her arms were fleshy again by this time. When the dough was kneaded to her satisfaction, she began to roll it out, using a painted metal cannister as a rolling pin. It reminded me of a thing my mother used to do: when she planted beans, she'd tread in the soil with her boot and roll it flat with an old tin barrel.

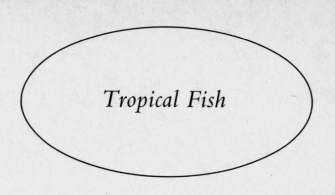

Tropical Fish

JOHN SPARROW IS dying.

Coming to the farm bungalow in the heat of early July, John Sparrow's old friends notice the changes. Large John has shrunk, under the candlewick cover, to sparrow. The hand he gives each of them to shake (always polite, John, always correct) is bird bone. Then in the kitchen, where his wife Mary makes tea or squash as they prefer, she shows them her new microwave oven. It tells digital time. As they stand and admire it, the blue numbers flick on. Time is passing for John Sparrow, but at least he's going rich.

His bed is near a window. He can still raise his head and see his acres, his single-minded land running flat to the sky. Harvest is coming. His wheat's the colour of buff board. John Sparrow nods at it: good land, good decisions. Once he farmed temperamental stuff, mucky stuff: soft fruit, chickens, a jersey herd. Then he sold the cows and the poultry and tore out the raspberry canes and ordered his arable seed. He made way for it. He bulldozed his hedges and cut down the ash and sycamore and filled in the clay ponds. With no obstacles in its way, his seed grew strong and straight. Yet it needed more room. John Sparrow walked the boundaries of his farm and sized up the pastures of his neighbours and sized up their struggles. Solicitors were engaged. Contracts passed to John Sparrow in buff envelopes. His seed, legitimised, marched on.

Now, he's leaving it. Mary Sparrow gets out the electric carver and slices bread for him. White bread and packet soups are what he tries to eat. Reared in a backward place, he's dying a modern death.

On this hot, dusty day, Bob Sparrow, John's only child, waits for the London train.

Bob Sparrow is the height his father once was, with his father's broad nose and the smile of his mother, furtive and sweet. At thirty, unmarried yet, Bob Sparrow's a fortnight from his twentieth harvest and days, perhaps, from his inheritance. His back is broad, his elbows fleshy, his belly in its leisurewear soft and fat. With his smart sneakers, with his briefcase full of catalogues, he looks like a rep. His nails are clean. He stands and waits and stares at the railway lines that shimmer. He fondles the change in his pocket. Easy, says his stance. Easy, says this nonchalant jingling of money.

On the train, he buys a four-pack and gets out his brochures. He spreads them around: sprayer arms, ten-row planters, water throwers, combines, bailers, tractors and ploughs. Two old farmers drinking tea stare across the aisle at the pictures. Bob Sparrow catches them staring, as if at pornography. He folds the shiny catalogues away and sits holding his paper cup, his face turned towards the fields.

He's on his way to an exhibition, *Agripower '87*. MIP is the dying John Sparrow's most cherished philosophy: Machinery is Profit. And the son, Bob Sparrow, is obedient to the mind which saw the folly of the dairy herd, the waste of the raspberry fields, the mind which altered the landscape. MIP. This year, the investment is large and the farm is a company, Sparrow Holdings Ltd. The old men drinking tea mumble in lost voices. And the Norfolk flatlands pass and vanish, minced up by the train.

Bob Sparrow leans his head against the hot window and daydreams of flying. He's never seen the Sparrow land from the air, but he can imagine its symmetry, his good ditches squaring it off on a neat grid. He'd like to own a plane. He wants to put himself above the land and look down. His mind puts up a windsock one field from the garden where the widow, Mary, will go patiently in circles with her Flymo. The sock struts tall above the tarmac runway, going east-west away from the silos. The wind hurtles in from the east. Easy. He's airborne in seconds. The oaks – the few that remain – are in seconds small. Bob Sparrow smiles and feels pleased with life's arrangement. John Sparrow walked on his patched and sculptured land and saw how it could be straightened. Soon, the old man will lie on his back, his nose pressed up to the clay, and he, the rich son, will walk above it.

Near London, Bob Sparrow finishes the beer. His belly feels bloated and his understanding diminished as the train goes slowly into the poor suburbs, Ilford, Seven Kings, Maryland, Stratford. He turns inwards from the grimy flats, turns his back on them and gets out his catalogues. 'Do the sums before you buy,' old John advises. 'Outlay versus man hours saved. Work it out.' And always Mary nods proudly, remembering a drudgery time, water saved in a butt, sheets boiled in a copper, yet one day confuses her men and surprises herself by asking: 'What are the hours saved for?'

'Sitting,' replies John.

'Flying,' Bob wants to say.

'I think you've all forgotten,' says Mary.

Bob Sparrow gets out of the train and smells the trapped air of the station. Above his head, glaziers are painstakingly repairing ancient structures. Bob only glances at this work and hurries to the underground. Stepping up into sunlight again at Earls Court, he finds himself moving with a crowd towards the exhibition centre. This crowd annoys him. The eager people. He'd expected to be part of a chequebook élite. 'Vision,' John Sparrow is fond of saying, 'needs space.'

His orders placed (orders for machinery John Sparrow will not see), Bob moves to Stand 56. The small, single-engined white plane sits on an area of plastic grass. Bob is invited by the salesmen to inspect the housing where the spray chemicals in their cylinders are clamped. The dummy cylinders are white like the plane.

He climbs, then, into the cockpit. ('Doddle to fly, Sir, these, Sir.') From the pilot's seat he feels tall at last above the milling crowds. Only the instrument panel dismays him. How many man hours lie between this moment and his vision of his airstrip? 'Easy, eh?' says the salesman, grinning above his white shirt. Teach me, Bob wants to say. 'Land in a field with these. Land anywhere, near enough,' says the salesman. And Bob nods and thinks of his mother alone and going in little circles with her mower and turning her flat face and waving up. 'Next year,' he says. 'I'll be in a position then.'

So he moves out into the hurry of five o'clock and is caught by another tide of people going from offices to trains and buses. Though he half intends staying in the herd that pushes along towards the underground station, he drops out of it and goes into a pub where he orders a pint and a pie. He takes these to a leather bench and feels, as he sits, a deep weariness with the day. Though he thinks he will telephone the bungalow, he knows he won't go home tonight.

He talks to no one. He goes once to the payphone. The payphone is broken. He orders more beer. In the bungalow, Mary will be plugging in the carver, measuring water for the soup granules. 'Will the lad be home?' John Sparrow will ask. Beer is sad stuff when John Sparrow is dying.

Bob goes back to the bar and orders whisky. The barman is Irish. 'Storm comin',' he announces. Bob nods and pays and goes back to his corner. And within a very few minutes, the sun at his back on the thick pub window goes and he hears thunder.

Not wanting to be trapped by the rain, remembering Mary sitting on her own with the telly while John snores and snarls his way into his invalid's sleep, he swallows the whisky, puts on his jacket and goes out into the street. Lights are on in Turkish take-aways, in pizza parlours: night starting in a foreign place. The huge storm moves in from the west, low over the airport.

Bob Sparrow hurries. The place he chooses has no hotel sign, only a hand-inked card, VACANCIES. The woman who opens the door is fifty and thick-waisted and she holds a small dog in her arms.

'We used,' she says as she walks up the stairs, 'to breed champions.'

'Champion dogs?' Bob asks.

'In this house,' she says, 'we used to exhibit.'

The room she shows him is carpeted and large and painted amber. 'There's this one,' says the woman, her stubby hand on the metal door handle, 'or if you find the tanks disturbing, there's another one I let out at the back, but smaller.'

'Tanks?' says Bob.

'Yes,' and she nods towards the wall facing the bed, 'the fish.'

Bob walks past her into the room. It has a musty smell that reminds him of the smell of the silos. There are three aquaria, dimly lit, arranged with stones and coral and fern. 'The thing is,' says the woman, 'they're not silent. It's the aeration.'

'Yes,' says Bob and glances from the fish tanks to the window, against which the rain begins to hurtle.

'They need to breathe,' says the woman and for the first time smiles tenderly at Bob. 'Some find it company.'

That night, John Sparrow dies in his bed.

Mary straightens the candlewick counterpane and sits with a little lamp on and tries to imagine her future, but her future seems flat. John Sparrow imagined his flat, featureless land, but he was tall in it. Where he went, Mary's eye followed.

So blind and cold in the landscape does Mary feel now that she creeps from the room and goes to the kitchen to boil milk for a hot drink. The blue digits of the oven clock flick on: 2:41. She waits and stares. 2:42. She thinks of her son.

The storm over London has moved on. Bob Sparrow wakes and stares at the ghostly light of the fish tanks and his head throbs. The bubbles rise and sigh. His tired eye becomes a swimmer and inquisitive swift visions pass into his mind. The bodies of the fish are soft, delicate as a brain. They're supple and fragile and streaming with colour and light. And Bob Sparrow remembers a day in summer when he creeps in secret in the jungle of raspberry canes and pops his eye through a dark gap in the leaves and sees a burst of red where the fruit hang. His nimble child's brain marvels and his child's hand pushes up and cups the berries and he squashes them on his tongue. And he darts on up the row, where the patterning of light and leaf is intricate and restless, always changing and moving, yet always there. He runs, playing games with the shadows and the raspberry field is beautiful and his soft limbs running are the most beautiful things of all.

Bob Sparrow snaps on the bedside lamp. For an instant, all the fish are still, as if immobilised by an electric shock. He looks away from them. The lamp casts a corn-coloured glow on the unfamiliar room. He searches in his briefcase for aspirin, swallows two, then lies on his back looking at the square ceiling. He doesn't glance again at the fish and tries not to listen to the sighing of the oxygen in the water. The throbbing in his head gradually ceases, but he can't sleep. He turns out the light and covers his face with his pillow. As time passes, he sees daylight at its edges and thinks of the dawn breaking on the rim of his land and of the harvest to come. His brain gathers it. His hard brain like a safe stores it and locks it. And nothing moves.

In the morning, the fifty-year-old woman cooks sausages for him and shows him her dog trophies. Bob Sparrow is polite. He admires the ugly trophies and then, as he's leaving, asks without interest why she keeps the fish.

'Well,' she says, 'they're a feature. Tropical fish are a feature.'

'Do you know their origins?' asks Bob, and the woman shrugs.

'I don't think those ever had origins,' she says. 'Or they might have done. In fact, I think they did because they're tropical, pet. But I've forgotten. It's the kind of thing you just forget.'

On the Monday that follows Bob Sparrow's return is old John's funeral. Mary's face at the graveside is white and still.

A year or so from this date, Bob Sparrow buys a light aircraft and beneath its elegant fins sees, to his satisfaction, his land become small: a square.

La Plume de Mon Ami

O N AN APRIL THURSDAY, Maundy Thursday in Gerald's Letts Diary, Gerald strolled in his city suit through the lunchtime crowds in Covent Garden and saw, through the window of an expensive shop, Robin buying knitwear. Until this moment – Robin, moving towards a full-length mirror with a beige and burgundy cardigan held tenderly against his shoulders, glances up, and his round blue eyes that haven't faded with time behold, through the artful display of home-knitted jerseys on wooden poles, Gerald looking in – Gerald and Robin hadn't met for twenty years. If they sometimes thought about each other, or had a dream in which the other appeared, or sent, on impulse, a Christmas card, they also knew that their friendship belonged too delicately to the past to survive the present or the future. They doubted they would ever meet again.

Gerald, at thirty-eight, was a tall, powerfully fashioned man, with a fleeting, blazing smile of touching emptiness. Robin, at forty-two, was neat-waisted, springy, very hesitantly balding, small. As they sighted each other, as if through an ancient, long-discarded pair of binoculars, both knew unerringly what the other would see: their separate mortality. Both felt, on the same instant, sweet sadness. Gerald smiled and walked into the shop. Robin, still holding to his chest the burgundy cardigan, moved neatly towards him and silently embraced him.

Because it was lunchtime and because, as Gerald neared

forty, he had become an innocently gourmandising man, he prolonged this meeting with Robin by the space of a meal, during which they discussed – very gently, so as not to lay on this fugitive encounter a feeling of heaviness – the past. That night, they went to their separate homes on different sides of London and began to remember it.

Gerald liked to remember things chronologically: cause and effect; beginning, middle and end. So he started by remembering the play – the Crowbourne school production of *Antony and Cleopatra*, in which he'd played an acclaimed Antony and in which at the last minute, because of the appendectomy of a dark-browed boy called Nigel Peverscombe, Robin had played a petulant Cleopatra. Hand in hand with his memories of his Crowbourne Antony went Gerald's memories of Palomina, his first woman.

Robin preferred to remember more selectively, starting with days, or even individual moments when he'd been happy or at least carefree, and only then proceeding, holding fast to the rim of his duvet in his dark and reassuring room, to those other times when he'd begun to see himself as a clown, a fool, a player in a tragedy even. He managed, however, a rueful smile. His life since that time hadn't been disagreeable. Certainly not tragic. Next term, he was taking over as Housemaster at Shelley, Crowbourne's premier house.

Gerald remembers staring, smiling as he bows, beyond the hot flood of the stage lights on their scaffolding, at the dark space above the heads of the audience, and feeling the future touch him lightly and beckon him out. School is over. He is eighteen and a man. Palomina is out there, applauding. Ahead is the summer. No child's beach holiday with his mother and father and his two baby sisters, but a journey this year, a man's adventure, two months of travel before the start of the Oxford term. He wants to applaud with the audience. Applaud his good fortune, his youthfulness, his potency. He wants to shout. 'Bravo!' cheer the Upper Sixth, sitting at the back. Gerald and Robin move forwards, separating themselves from the rest of the cast. The clapping and stamping is thunderous.

Gerald shivers with ecstasy and hope. He smiles his captivating smile. 'We did it,' Robin whispers. And Gerald's wellspring of optimism is turned to admiration and affection for Robin, the young teacher, his Oxford already in the past, producer of the play and, finally, its bravest star. '*You* did it, Robin,' he corrects.

He remembers nothing about the school after that night. Not the farewells, nor the packings of trunks, not even the last singing of the school song. It fell away from him and he cast it aside. It was strange for him to imagine, as he sat on the deck of the channel steamer with Robin and watched the English coast become thin and insubstantial that Robin would be returning to Crowbourne in September. Why live through Oxford and get to know the proper world and then go back? I will never do this, he promises himself, I will never go back to Crowbourne except as the father of future Crowbournians. Robin will teach them and remember me. In his repetitious life it will be me, not my sons, who will count.

It's chilly on the boat, windy and grey. Near Dieppe, it gets rough and Gerald and Robin sit huddled up in their coats. Robin produces a hip flask of brandy. The silver mouth of the flask has a warm and bitter taste. They don't talk much.

At Dieppe, their legs unsteady after the long boat crossing, they lug their suitcases to the Paris train. This was before the days of backpacks and weightless, shiny bags. For two months, they carried those heavy cases around, re-labelling them for each new stage of the journey. They were scraped and scratched and dented and buffeted and sat on. Arriving back at Victoria, they seemed like the sad trophies of a battle. Gerald can't remember what became of his suitcase, but he remembers the look and feel of it in his cheap Paris room, opening it and laying out on the shiny coverlet a clean shirt and the kind of striped jacket that used to be called 'casual'. Men's clothes. He'd become a man. Now Robin would show him France. All the places he'd learned about he would see and touch, wearing his casual clothes. With Robin he walks out into the Paris night. Robin leads them unerringly to a noisy, whitely lit

73

brasserie and advises Gerald, 'Have *pied de porc*. They know how to cook it here.' When the meal arrives, Gerald stares at the trotter on his plate and thinks, good, from now on I shall seek out the unfamiliar. That night, he has a dream he's snuffling for truffles.

Of course, says Robin to himself, as if in answer to a question, I remember Paris! We were in the *sixième*. The hotel proprietor wore an eyepatch. I had room No. 10. We didn't go into each other's rooms, but stood only on the thresholds. Paris was the threshold of the journey. Gerald wore clean, smart clothes that got dirtier as the summer went on. He seemed large in that French city. I was a better size for Paris. He was golden and greedy and loud. I disliked him, suddenly. He tried to make me get up early to take him to the Louvre, but I didn't want his enthusiasm for the pictures, I wanted to go on my own and spend some time with the Cézannes. I felt in need of foliage and quiet. I said, 'Go on your own, Gerald. I've seen the Louvre.' I walked in the Luxembourg Gardens where, every time I've been there I seem to see a nun, and started writing my diary. I'd arranged to meet Gerald there and he came running at me, waving like a lunatic. I blushed for him. 'Leave me here,' I wanted to tell him, 'go on on your own.' But he sat down and began to chivvy me about – of all people – Rubens. 'I can't stand Rubens,' I told him. So he shut up and sighed and began to kick dusty pebbles like a boy. Yes, I disliked him then. Some nuns passed and he smiled at them. I started to write down 'N' in my diary for every nun I saw. I decided they were bad omens.

Another thing I didn't like about Gerald then was his piety. It was a false piety, born out of his successes at Crowbourne and his romantic love of the girl, Palomina. He displayed it, though, in all the grand churches, Notre Dame, the Sainte Chapelle, the Sacré Coeur. Of these three, only the Sainte Chapelle is quiet and the other two mill with tourists in ugly clothes, exhibiting their own brand of false piety by lighting candles for people far away. Watching them, I try to imagine the names of the people getting the candles. Over the years, the names have changed. Now, they're mainly Japanese: Kyoko, Nukki,

Yami, Go. Then, twenty years ago, they were American: Candice, Wilbur, Nancy-Anne, Buck. They disgusted me. Gerald's lighting of candles disgusted me. I was, then as now, a very unsentimental man. I saw several N's in the three churches that day. N's look as if they're always whispering to Jesus and I can't abide these private conversations. They could be talking to God about me.

Of our three nights in Paris, I prefer to remember the third. We are asked – a prearranged date – to dine with Monsieur and Madame de Bladis, friends of Gerald's parents. Gerald refers to these people as 'The Bladders'. Brushing our cuffs, shining our shoes with paper hankies, we take the Métro to Neuilly, where the Bladders have a *maison particulière*. 'She's rather fun,' Gerald tells me, 'she has a sense of humour.' And the thought flits into me like a bat: do riches alter the jokes you make, the things you laugh at? I feel poor on the stuffy Métro. For the first time since leaving England, I'm at peace with Gerald's size and air of wealth. I decide, on the morrow, to grow a beard. My first beard. I don't tell Gerald my decision. I'll let him notice it himself.

The de Bladis house is emphatically grand. Porcelain blackamoors hold on their turbaned heads a marble table in the hall. Madame de Bladis is chiffoned, pearled and rouged and sweeps down her cascading staircase like a dancer. She leads us to the roof, where there is a canopied garden, complete with a tiny fountain, the noise of which creates in my own bladder a perpetual yet not unexciting desire to piss. 'Gerald, Gerald,' she says in her soft French voice, 'you are getting so beautiful. Why don't we have a daughter to offer you?!' Gerald is quieter here, awed by the roof garden, very beautiful indeed. And it's to me, in his shyness of these people, that Gerald turns – for encouragement, for the right word in his hesitant A-Level French, for confirmation of an idea or an opinion. I become the teacher again and the old intimacy we had for the weeks of the *Cleopatra* rehearsals and then lost as we arrived in France, returns. As Gerald's friend, I am made welcome. We are served *anguillettes* – a kind of minuscule eel I've never eaten before or since – as a first course. All along the

75

roof, as the sky deepens, pink lanterns are lit. Above and between these, tilting back my happy head, I see the stars. 'Your friend is smiling,' says Madame de Bladis, 'I like this.'

Gerald remembers a feeling of admiration, of envy almost for Monsieur de Bladis. A bank to run, a sumptuous house to own, a pretty wife with a plump, high-sitting bosom to be deliciously unfaithful to – these earthly rewards could be worth striving for. I will, he decides, watching the plash-plash of the fountain, watching the gloved hands of the servant who brings a hot chocolate soufflé, try to make a success of things. Oxford and the Law. The route is straight. I'm on my marks. Yet there's a little time, such as now, sitting on a roof in Neuilly on a warm night, to be *savoured* before the race begins. Even Robin is allowing himself to savour this night. He's stopped feeling cross. He's started to enjoy himself. And tomorrow we go south, as far as the Loire.

'Ah,' says Robin, 'ah, yes, yes,' as we see, admirable and stately above the town, the Château de Blois. And I know that this little lisp of pleasure he lets sigh conceals his abundant knowledge of French and Italian architectural caprice, that he will guide me through the complexities of the building in the same delighted way he guided me through Shakespeare's verse. He's twenty-two. How has all this knowledge been crammed into him? I feel as empty of history as a willow bat. As Robin prances round the dark well of the François Ier staircase, he murmurs, 'Brabante, you see. Used by Il Boccadoro. Note the balustrade. Shallow relief ornamentation. Very Brabante.' And I want to mock him. 'Very Brabante, Robin? Really?' But I don't. I let him bound on, gazelle-like in his light-treading reverence for stone, and I am invaded with my longing for Palomina. I want her there and then on the staircase. Her pubic hair is lightly brown. I want to tangle my life in her little brown briar bush. I lean on the balustrade and look down into the sunshine. A couple below me seem small and I'm dizzy with my Palomina-lust. 'Gerald!' Robin calls sternly, 'come on!'

The *pension* Robin has found near the station is poor.

Outside my window is a vegetable garden where an old man works till dusk, hoeing and coughing and lighting thin cigarettes. His cough wakes me in the morning. The place has a cold, green painted dining room where, for dinner, we're served a watery consommé followed by some lukewarm chicken. We don't dare ask for vegetables, though in the garden I've seen peas and beans and marrows, but a dish of these arrives long after we've eaten the chicken. '*Je m'excuse*,' says a thin, vacant-eyed waitress as she plonks the dish down. We eat the beans obediently and talk about money. We should economise on rooms, says Robin. All right, I say.

I've begun to worry about how, in all the weeks to come, I'll ever get my underpants washed. At school, you put out all your dirty clothes on your bed on a Friday morning and made a list of them and they were returned to you, washed and ironed, the following week. Who washed and ironed them exactly, or where, I'm not able to say. I've never washed any clothes myself ever in my life, though I've heard there's something called Tide you're supposed to use. Can one buy Tide in France, or is it called something else? '*Marée*', for instance? I sense, by the set of Robin's nostrils as he plans our next day's visit to Chambord, that he's become too unearthly for these kind of questions. But I rather love and admire his enthusiasm for buildings and feel pleased I asked him to come with me. I notice, in the cold light of the green dining room, that he's unshaven for the second day running. Is he, I wonder, going to model himself on more intrepid travellers than us? Scott, for instance? Or Alfred Russell Wallace? But I don't ask him this. We go to bed rather early, me to write to Palomina, he to write his diary.

Extract from Robin's Diary. July 31st 1964.
Ch. of Blois v. calming. Size has a tranq. effect on me. Renaiss. arch. seems so sure of itself, so sophisticatedly playful, nothing *mean* in it. Not hard to imag. my life in a turret.

G's arms and face are getting quite brown from sitting about. I think there's a kind of impatience in him to get

77

south. I shall rein him back – he my horse, me his chevalier!

This room is mournful.

Saw two NN at the Ch.

Chambord tomorrow, hooray.

Extract from Gerald's letter to Palomina. July 31st 1964.
My darling Palomina,

One week since I saw you. I miss you, my darling. Do you miss me? I miss you so much. Please write Poste Restante to Avignon or Nice.

I saw a fine Renaissance staircase today. I missed you on it. Do you miss me on staircases?

At Chambord, Robin remembers, he was still in his carefree time. After Blois and now here, he's becoming a François Ier admirer. At Chambord, the great king had a river, the Cusson, diverted to his castle's feet. Robin lies on the sunny grass, eating bread and a carton of brawn salad, and imagines all the everlasting things he would like to re-route towards his master's cottage at Crowbourne: the Spanish steps, Michelangelo's David, Cézanne's jungles, Dylan Thomas's house-high hay, the golden vestments of Saladin. He's aware, with his face tipped up to the blue sky, of the Loire valley as a kind of cradle where he and the grand houses can quietly affirm their remoteness from the modern, the discordant, the utilitarian and the plebeian. Tiny orchids, wild as weeds, grow near his head. *Bliss.* Order and beauty and grace. *Blissful.* He doesn't move. Gerald gets up and struts around, taking photographs. Robin thinks of the frail King Charles IX who would hunt in this park for ten hours at a stretch and blow his hunting horn till his throat bled. Gerald is daring like this with his limbs. In the high-jump, he'd hurl his big body at the bar. 'Run, Gerald!' Robin wants to call to him. He loves to see him run. But he's gone off somewhere with his camera and Robin is alone.

He's gone off, in fact, to try to buy a stamp for his letter to Palomina. He thinks the little kiosk where they sell postcards and slides might also sell him a stamp, or rather several stamps, because he plans to write to Palomina a lot. He's heavy with his Palomina-lust and writing to her assuages it. '*Ah non, Monsieur,*' snaps the kiosk woman, '*nous ne sommes pas un bureau de poste.*'

'*Pardonne . . .*' says Gerald, '*pardonnez-moi.*'

'*Allez!*' says the woman with a sniff. It's as if he'd asked for a French letter. He blushes.

Robin remembers the Avignon train. It's the Boulogne night train, but there are no sleepers, nor even any seats. It's crammed with Parisians going south, sitting wearily shoulder to shoulder, like in wartime. He and Gerald stand at a corridor window and as the darkness comes, they begin to sense the air getting warmer. They're lulled by the thought of a lavender sunrise in Provence. They lie down in the corridor with their heads on their suitcases and doze and all the shoulder-to-shoulder people lean and nod and pull down their blinds and a general tiredness overcomes the train.

The train stops several times, but no one seems to get on or off. Robin sits up and stares at the names of stations: Vienne, Valence, Montélimar . . . Gerald seems to be sleeping soundly, enfolding his suitcase like a lover, his long legs in creased trousers heavy and still on the dirty floor. Robin takes an old cardigan he used to wear at Oxford out of his own case and covers Gerald's shoulders with this.

At six o'clock at Avignon-Fontcouverte, where the air is chilly and white with a dense mist, they stumble out, shivering, and follow the upright Parisians to a clean, new-seeming station restaurant serving croissants in their hundreds and large cups of coffee.

Now, tasting this good, hot coffee, they feel the traveller's awareness of deprivation and blessing, warmth after cold, shelter after storm. They don't talk, but each is privately happy. And they're south at last. Along the station platform, a hazy yellow sun disperses the mist and starts to glimmer on the plane trees. Gerald's hair is tousled, giving him a shaggy, unruly look that Robin finds disturbing. On his cheek is a pink blotch, where it's lain pressed against the suitcase lid.

Gerald remembers how they walked through suburbs where buildings were sparse then, past plumbers' yards and garages and a vast, empty hippodrome to the centre of the city, lugging the heavy cases. Buses passed them, taking people to work. Gerald suggested they should get on one of the buses, but Robin said no, he wanted air. So they walked till the city streets started to narrow round them and the Pope's Palace was there above them, then sat down at a pavement café and saw from the milling crowds and fluttering banners and flags that Avignon was in the middle of a festival. 'There'll be a problem with rooms,' Robin said, and in the hot sun Gerald felt tired and sleepy. Then he remembered that at the central post office there might be a letter from Palomina, and wanted to run to the letter and press the envelope against his nose, breathing in the translucent airmail sentences of his woman.

'I've got to go to the post office,' he said, getting up. 'I'll be back in half an hour.' And he darted away, leaving Robin sitting on his own with the luggage.

The room is shadowy, remembers Robin, in a kind of well of buildings which shoulder off the light. There's a double bed with a hard bolster and no pillows. The bedcoverings feel heavy and chill.

They're lucky to find the room. All the cheap places have *complet* signs up. This is the last vacant room in the last hotel . . .

On either side of the bed, back to back they lie in the early evening and try to sleep. Robin is acutely aware of Gerald's breathing. On a rusty washbasin near the bed stands an orange packet of Tide Gerald has bought. In the absence of any letter from Palomina with which to pass a secret hour before dinner, he's washed out all his underpants. They're hung on a rail at the side of the basin and drip steadily onto the lino floor. He's naked in the bed except for a short sleeved T-shirt, and as well as his breathing Robin is aware of his firm, round buttocks very near to his own, and feels, for the first time since the night of *Cleopatra*, a fatal stab of desire. He buries his face in the bolster and forces himself to remember the dark, Italianate features of the girl Gerald loves, Palomina, four years older than him, staying *au pair* with Gerald's family, helping with the baby sisters. She's a plump girl, not beautiful, but wide-eyed and wayward-seeming, with a mane of brown frizzy hair. The antithesis of blond, handsome Gerald. Yet pious like him, probably, with an exaggerated, lying Catholic piety. Confessing after he fucks her.

The room's above a café in the tiny, hemmed-in square. At the window, Robin can hear swallows and the sound of tables being laid for dinner.

Extract from Gerald's letter to Palomina. August 8th 1964.
My dearest Palomina,

I've written to you almost every day. When we got here (to Avignon) I went straight to the PTT and God I was so miserable when there was no letter from you. It was so beastly, and I began to ask myself jealous questions: have you found another boy? Please reassure me, my darling, that you still love me. I feel like dying. This dying feeling is so horrible I think I must break my promise and visit you when you get to your parents' house on the 23rd. Please say I can. I'm in torment without your breasts.

Extract from Robin's Diary. August 8th 1964.

Prog. into Avig. is through draperies announcing a music and theatre festival. So no rooms of course. Boulevards choc-a-bloc with German youth. Thighs etc.

Tourists are teeming coarsefish. G. and I try to behave like surface feeders, Mayfly gourmets. This will be diffic. here. We're sharing a room, for reasons of econ. mainly. G. is washing his knickers in Tide.

Had a dream last night in the train corridor Aunt M. was dead. Hope she isn't. She's the only intell. woman my family produced.

Avig. teeming with NNs.

Lost count after 9. Bad sign.

NB. P. des Papes looks monolithic, just right for the Church, but wrong for me. Adieu la renaissance.

Gerald remembers waiting in Avignon for the letter that never came. Day after day, he goes to the central post office and says his name, Gerald Willoughby. *Je crois que vois avez une lettre pour moi, Gerald Willoughby.*

'*Non,*' they say, '*non, rien pour vous.*'

He dreads it then: *rien pour vous.* You have nothing, Gerald, *are* nothing without the embrace of Palomina.

The city is hot, choked, dusty. They follow the tourists in a line up the ramparts of the Pope's Palace. The wind brings gusts of litter. One night, they sit on planks to hear the voice of Gérard Philippe reciting Victor Hugo at a Son et Lumière performance, and the vast walls of the Palace are lit with strange violet light, behind which the sky seems violet and the bats like black musical notes, bodiless, flying to nowhere. They return penniless and sorrowful to their room. Robin's wallet has been stolen. They spend the next day telephoning Lloyds Bank and Thomas Cook and Robin's mother in Swindon and wait, with the letter that doesn't come, for money to be sent to them.

They walk out to the famous bridge, the Pont St Bénézet, and the Rhône is slow, majestic and green as the Amazon. Gerald remembers the blue of the Loire and feels the change in river colour to be one among very many confusions: Palomina's silence, the mood of sadness that seems to have settled on Robin, the feeling of heaviness this city imparts. For the first time since leaving England, he's lonely.

Robin spends hours at the Musée Calvet. He tries to perceive where, in the Daumier drawings, amid the torrent of lines, the artist has changed his mind. Unconsciously, he's seeking out the rage in the pictures, yet hoping to be calmed by them. He sits down very frequently on the hard *banquettes* and the image of Gerald's turned back in the bed comes unasked-for into his mind. And he looks round and sees Gerald some way off, staring at the paintings, but not *entering* them, as Robin does, just vacantly gazing, unmoved, untouched.

On the eighth day in Avignon replacement traveller's cheques arrive and Gerald re-packs his underpants which have dried stiff and powdery, not quite like they were in the days of the school laundry. 'I expect there's a knack to washing, is there?' he asks, as he examines the French writing on the Tide packet. Robin merely shrugs and touches his new beard, in which there seem to be little clusters of grey. It's only since the night of Son et Lumière that he's stopped answering all of Gerald's questions. Very often, the boy looks hurt.

The absence of an airmail letter from Palomina is hurting. All Gerald can think of now is getting to the central post office in Nice. He can *see* the letter in its little metal compartment. He can *see* Palomina's bunched-up continental writing. Yet the thought that Palomina has stopped loving him is giving him pains in his bowel. 'I feel strange,' he tells Robin, as they climb onto a hot, mid-afternoon train and sit down opposite two nuns, 'I feel weak.'

He leans his head against the burning glass of the train window and closes his eyes. The train's crowded with young people, German, Dutch, American. The seats opposite the nuns were the only two available. '*Milano!*' asks a big Italian with hairy thighs, as he pushes past with his rucksack. '*Non,*' says Robin.

The Italian looks distractedly up and down the train. A tin mug, strung onto a canvas loop of his haversack, almost bangs the wimple of the outer nun, who lowers her pale face and folds her arms. '*Questo treno. A Milano, non?*' the Italian asks the nuns. '*Nice!*' they whisper, in unison. '*Ah fucki shiti!*' he says, seizing a hank of springy hair, and pushes himself towards the door, arms held high, like a wader. Robin smiles, liking the horror on the faces of the Sisters. 'God!' says an American girl, 'wait till I tell Myrna I touched Gérard Philippe. She'll die!'

The train starts to move. Cool air comes in above Gerald's blond head. Gerald remembers, on this train, the feeling of becoming very ill. He remembers falling in and out of a deep and sickly sleep and dreaming of the sea. He remembers the nuns looking up at him under their pale brows. He remembers Robin soaking his handkerchief with Evian water and giving this to him and, when it touches his head, feeling cold to his marrow. 'I'm sorry, Robin, so sorry . . .' he keeps repeating. And he walks

83

past all the hot Dutch and German bodies to a foul-smelling toilet and shits his soul out into the stained pan. There's no paper in the lavatory. With shaky hands, Gerald pulls his wallet from the shorts that lie round his feet and wipes himself with two dry cleaners' tickets saying 2prs gr flannels and 1 blue blzr. His school clothes. Swilled away somewhere between Brignoles and Vidauban.

Over Nice, where they arrive towards six o'clock, rolls a gigantic thunderstorm. Outside the crowded station, the rain begins to teem and Gerald's enfeebled brain wants to cry for England and familiarity and shelter. He's forgotten the letter waiting for him at the central post office. He's incapable of Palomina-lust. He can barely walk. Sweat is running off him like the rain off the station roof. 'Stay here,' says Robin, sitting Gerald on a bench with the luggage. 'I'll go and find us a room.'

And he watches hopelessly as Robin darts out into the forecourt, where people mill and shout and wait for taxis and buses. NICE COTE D'AZUR says a white and blue sign, and Gerald remembers that they are, at last, by the sea. Yet the bench towards which his head soon falls and rests smells of city soot. He puts a limp arm round the suitcases and longs for Robin to return.

It's dark by the time a Citroën taxi takes them into the *vieille ville*. The storm has moved inland and is hurtling far off, over the mountains. The sea's calm in the big bay, silvery in its glut of reflected light. 'What a show,' Gerald mumbles, 'Nice is.'

Their room is an attic. Robin remembers the pigeon's noisy existence on an iron window bar and the depths of quiet falling away below them into a courtyard. For most of his life, at least two or three times a year, in a dream, he's returned to this room with its view of gutters and chimney pots and balconies and washing. The hotel is called the Jean Bart. There's one lavatory every other floor. In the room below them an eighty-year-old Finnish woman struggles with the stairs. She tells Robin she's well known in her country for her translations of D.H. Lawrence. Robin feels light and happy among the roofs.

Twice a day, he carries bouillon and bread up all the flights of dark steps to Gerald's bed. He and a pert maid tidy the room around their golden invalid, who is humble in his sufferings, cut down to size. For three days, Palomina isn't mentioned. At night, Robin and Gerald lie side by side in the dark and talk of going on into Italy. Robin writes a postcard to his mother in Swindon saying: Arr. Nice. Old Town v. congenial. Trust yr hip not playing up in hot weather. Blessings, Robin. Gerald sleeps. Robin unwinds the sellotape from the Tide packet and washes, with gentle attention, his patient's underwear and his own. He dries the clothes at the window where the male pigeons wear their showy tailfeathers like long kilts.

Gerald remembers his resurrection on the fourth day. He's standing in the PTT. The building has a vaulted roof like a church. It's cool and dark. An Irish girl is weeping and being comforted by a friend she addresses as Dilly. 'Oh Jesus, Dilly,' she sobs, 'oh Dilly, Dilly . . .' And a pale PTT employee snaps, *'Monsieur Willuffby?'* and slides a glass grille open and pushes towards Gerald an airmail letter.

That night, as Robin and Gerald sit on a pavement in the *vieux port* and eat red mullet and a brilliant sunset the colour of the mullet tails descends on the cloudless evening, Robin takes out his postcard to his mother and adds, in angry schoolmaster's red biro, PS. Weather here lousy. Gerald looks helplessly from Robin's card to the sky and sighs. It's intolerable, Robin, he wants to say.

The house of Palomina's parents in the hills behind Ajaccio is remembered entirely differently by Gerald and Robin, the smell of the *maquis* and of the eucalyptus trees being the one sweet, sad memory common to both. Robin remembers the unpleasant feeling of grit under his bare feet on the tiled floors. Gerald remembers gliding on these same floors like a silky ghost to Palomina's bedroom door. Robin remembers the terror of finding himself, for the first time in his life, astride a horse. Gerald, on a bay mare, remembers the joy of it, and the blissful sight, not far in

85

front of him, of Palomina's bikini-clad buttocks going up and down on her Mexican saddle. Robin remembers the feeling, in these hard hills, in the shadow of the granite mountains, of becoming soft, boneless, vulnerable, too easily crushed and bruised, the feeling of helpless flesh. Gerald remembers arranging his big body next to Palomina's in the sunshine and letting his eyes wander in the topmost pinnacles of rock, and thinking, I could climb those. With my bare hands and wearing only my football boots, I could master the Monte d'Oro.

The storms have gone north. Over all of Corsica shimmers the breathless heat that seems, in Robin's brain, to suspend time, to make every day long and blinding and purposeless, a month of empty sabbaths, everyone and everything monotonously sighing and humming and burning.

The house sits on a small hill, itself contained in a wider valley hemmed in by the mountains. Below the hill is a stream, torrential in winter, now slow but cold and clear and full of minnows. Each evening, Robin comes down here and lowers his hectic head into the water and opens his eyes and sees in the green river his own foolish lovesick feet planted on the sand. He wishes it was autumn. In the crisp beginning of the new school year, there was purpose and dignity. In his diary, which he can hardly bear to write during this futile time, he makes plans to abandon Gerald and go on into Italy on his own. His writing in the diary is so bad, the language so truncated, he has trouble, some years later, deciphering what he wrote.

Extracts from Robin's Diary. August 24th – August 30th 1964. Miserab. arriv. G. so puffed up to see P. I cld wring his neck.

No car avail. So we're stuck in this idiotic 'ranch'. G. thinks he's Yul Brynner. Or worse.

G. gets me on a f. horse. Failure.

Lg to see some sights, even if it's only Napoleon's House.

Boredom.

P's mother, Jeanne, is an enig prd shallow persec woman. You sense no one loves her. We lnch in Ajacc. Then she show us the fam. tomb. Hideous. 4NN.

Alone today. G., P., and J. went riding. Allwd car. Saw N's house. Dispp. One gd portrait by Gros. Also Chap. Imp. Welcome brush with Renaiss. order. Coming out into the sun again, wanted to die.

Mst get to Italy. Flor. Siena. La bella Toscana. Je souffre. Je souffre. Dream again Aunt M. died. Buried her behind some frescoes.

For Gerald, this valley contains like a casket the precious possessions which are Palomina's ruby nipples, her amber arms. His body is a slow avalanche of desire, engulfing, obliterating. Palomina. Paradise. His blood enquires about nothing but the act of love on Palomina's single bed at dawn, before her mother is awake, before Robin comes sighing out of his dreams, before the sun has fallen across the shiny rumps of the horses in their dusty stables. He remembers a thin line of white six o'clock light coming under the shutters. Day. Everything in this coming day glitters with hope: the smile under the lipstick on the lips of Palomina's mother; the sun on his knuckles as he eats his breakfast melon; the silver of the shivery eucalyptus; the fatal, alluring, far-off blue of the horizon. *I'm in paradise.* He wishes that he was keeping a diary like Robin's, so that he could record each new ecstasy.

He's sharing a room with Robin. In the room are twin beds, covered with white Portuguese lace, a painted chest of drawers, an oak wardrobe, a blue and yellow china lamp and a dusty bit of rattan serving as a mat. This modest arrangement of furniture now contains the bountiful happiness of Gerald and the silent misery of Robin. As a kind of poultice on his wound, Robin remembers the room at the Jean Bart and the carrying of broth and Gerald's sweet gratitude. 'I'd have died if it wasn't for you, Robin,' he said. Now, in Corsica, with these two dark, thick-browed women and Gerald's fair hair going pale as honey, Robin feels he's dying. Not precisely of love, but of his own foolishness. He can live without Gerald. What he can't seem to manage is to live with him and yet without him.

'I know,' he says one night to Gerald, 'you'd probably like to stay on here. But there's a ferry back to Nice tomorrow and I think I'll get on it and then press on to Italy like we planned.'

'On your own?'

'Yes.'

'Don't you like it here? You don't like Palomina, do you?'

'I just want to get to Italy.'

'Don't you love the mountains? You love the river, don't you?'

'They're all right.'

'You mean it's churches and paintings and things you miss? But you saw Napoleon's House, didn't you. You liked that.'

'I want to leave, Gerald.'

'But we agreed, Robin, we'd have this holiday together.'

'I know.'

'So you can't just desert me. And, listen, Palomina's father's arriving tomorrow. We'll get taken to more things. He's a big wheel. The Tomasini family are big wheels here.'

I should, said Robin to himself, twenty years later, have left the next day. Why didn't I leave? Why did I do what Gerald wanted?

Obediently, he puts on a clean shirt and trims his startling beard for the return of André Tomasini. This man, who has made a lot of money by Corsican standards, arrives in an ancient Chevrolet and is accompanied by four slender-hipped young men, wearing medallions. These men are embraced by Palomina like brothers. Tomasini is a small, cruel-faced man, whose authority seems to reside in his thin-tipped Roman nose. He greets Gerald and Robin unsmilingly ('oh, I see, my daughter invited you, did she?'), covers Palomina's face with intimate kisses and

88

ignores his wife until she informs him that lunch is ready, when he bangs her bottom like a dinner gong.

They sit down to the meal. Tomasini begins a lengthy, superstitious grace, invoking the name of '*notre ancêtre illustre, Letitzia Ramolini, mère de l'Empereur*'. What this had to do with the eating of *saucisson* and trout remains, to this day, a mystery to Gerald, part of all that he suddenly couldn't understand. Now, the house where he's lived in ecstasy is invaded with conversation and gesture and innuendo and private knowledge from which he's deliberately excluded. Outside, the light is as fierce, the crickets as noisy, the horses as elegantly restless as on all previous days, yet Gerald knows – in Tomasini's patriarchal behaviour, in the reverently lowered eyes of Palomina, in the withdrawal of Jeanne's friendly conversation – that his status is altered. No matter if Palomina works *au pair* in his family, here it's only the Corsicans who count. The strangers are inferior. Gerald looks helplessly at Robin, who is eating his trout primly, in utter silence. He refuses to catch Gerald's eye. His lowered and impassive face is, the boy supposes, still dreaming hopelessly of Florentine marble. Fleetingly, he envies Robin his detachment.

'Who,' says Tomasini, as the meal ends, 'is coming riding with me this evening? Palomina?'

'Yes, Papa.'

There are four horses. Two of the young men are invited. Gerald thinks of Palomina's bouncing bottom and her mane of brown hair and stares with dismay at his mess of trout bones. Palomina and the young men have started to giggle at some private joke. Then the afternoon unfolds: Tomasini takes his wife to bed; Palomina and the young men and Gerald go down to the river. While the others play like children and splash about, Gerald sits on his towel and feels too large, his skin too pale, his hopes too serious. Robin goes and lies down on the Portuguese lace. He can hear, on the other side of the wall, Tomasini's brief and ritualised exertions. With a kind of weariness, he tugs out his diary and writes: NNN. Negative. Null. Nothing.

89

The following morning, Gerald wakes as usual at dawn. In this valley, the importance of each unfolding day seems to fatten with the sunrise. He stands with his eyes narrowed to the crack in the shutters and is filled with his own longing. The house is silent. Towards midnight, the young men drove away in the Chevrolet. Robin sleeps. Gerald's tall, brown body is twenty-six paces from Palomina's bed. He wants, in the touch of Palomina's stubby hand, to be forgiven his jealousy and restored to favour. He feels old – at the very centre of his life. The boy who played Antony is far off, left behind in his silly paper armour. Antony the man is here, clenching and unclenching his man's fist. He pulls on his shorts, glances at Robin's face made gentle and sad by sleep, and goes out into the dark passage. The tiled floor is icy under his feet. He's afraid. He thought love was easy, just as Latin verse and cricket and the worship of God were easy. Until yesterday, he thought this.

He's at Palomina's door. He opens it as slowly, as silently as he can. On the other mornings, her room has been dark, darkness his ally, shaping the room softly round him as he slipped under the thin sheet. Today, light startles him. He stares, his eyes wide. Palomina sits on her bed eating a nectarine and smiles at him. Juice from the fruit wets her chin. Not far from the bed, sitting in a wicker chair, wearing a towelling robe, is André Tomasini. Gerald draws in a breath, begins to back out of the room.

'Come in, come in, Gerald!' Tomasini calls kindly.

He hesitates, his hand on the door. Palomina sucks her nectarine. 'Come in and sit down,' says Tomasini. Gerald moves into the room and looks blankly at the tableau of father and daughter. Palomina looks at him wistfully, but her eyes are hard. 'Sit down,' says Tomasini again. He perches on a hard chair, where some of Palomina's clothes are strewn, smelling of sun oil and her ripe body.

'Now,' says Tomasini, 'don't look so alarmed, Gerald. We're not barbarians here, you know, we're not *banditi* like you English always suppose, but we like to get everything right for our families, you understand?'

'How do you mean, "right"?' says Gerald.

Palomina licks the nectarine stone. Tomasini lights a cigarette.

'My daughter is twenty-two,' says Tomasini. 'Do you think I want her to spend her life *au pair* in England?'

'No . . .'

'No. This is for learning a language, no more. She is twenty-two and she must have a future.'

'Of course she must . . .'

'Boys of eighteen do not marry.'

'I could –'

'No, no. Don't be silly. Boys of eighteen do not marry. Now, I think you have had some hospitality in this house from my wife, no?'

'Yes. Yes, we have . . .'

'Good. So you will tell your parents we made you welcome?'

'Yes . . .'

'Good. But this is enough. You understand?'

Gerald gapes. Palomina turns her head to the window. 'I think you understand,' says Tomasini, 'I think you're a clever boy, Gerald. I think you're going to do well at Oxford.'

'Sir, I –'

'And a boy who's going to do well at Oxford can understand what is being asked.'

'You want me to leave.'

'Of course. And your friend. You take the ferry today.'

Finding no words in him, Gerald merely nods. Palomina. Paradise. Over. She won't save him. He stares in silence at her as she puts down the nectarine stone and licks her fingers, one by one.

During the lunch in Covent Garden, Gerald said, lighting one of the cigarettes he was trying so hard to give up, 'I suppose our happiest time was after Corsica, in Italy.'

Robin, who didn't smoke, passed Gerald the ashtray.

91

'I've always,' he said, 'loved Italy. I always will, I expect.' And he smiled across the table at his friend, to whom it was pointless to say, no, Italy was worse than anything. All you thought about was that stupid Palomina. Standing in front of the David, even right there, I could still see it in you, your silly longing. It marred everything we did.

'I go to Nice sometimes,' Robin said, taking a toothpick out of a white china jar. 'Once I went to look at the Jean Bart.'

'The what?'

'The Jean Bart. Our hotel.'

'Was that what it was called?'

'Yes. It's still there. Our room's still there. The room where you were ill, remember?'

'Oh that was an awful time, wasn't it! Poor you. You were so kind to me. I remember you used to have these dreams about an aunt or someone you thought had died.'

'Aunt Mabel. Yes. She had died. She died the day we arrived in Ajaccio.'

'Oh, I'm sorry, Robin.'

'Yes. She was lovely. She's buried in Tintagel.'

'Tintagel?' said Gerald, raising an arm to summon a waiter. 'Can't say I've ever been there. Time to get the bill, do you think?'

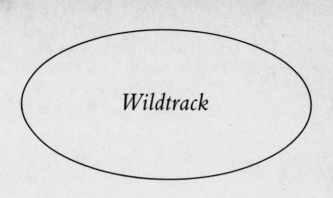

Wildtrack

MICKY STONE, WEARING camouflage, crouches in a Suffolk field, shielding his tape recorder from the first falling of snow. It's December. Micky Stone, who is approaching his fiftieth birthday, perfectly remembers touching his mother's fingers as she stood at the metal window of the cottage kitchen, watching snow fall. She was saying something. 'Isn't it quiet?' she was saying, but ten year-old Micky was deaf and couldn't hear.

Now, in the field, holding the microphone just above his head, he hears the sounds it gathers: the cawing of rooks, the crackle of beech branches as the birds circle and return. He hears everything perfectly. When he looks down at the tape machine, he hears his head turning inside his anorak hood.

Seven operations there were. Mrs Stone, widowed at thirty-five, sat in the dark of the hospital nights and waited for her son to wake up and hear her say, 'it's all right.' And after the seventh operation she said, 'it's all right now, Micky,' and he heard. And sound entered his mind and astonished him. At twelve, he asked his mother: 'who collects the sound of the trains and the sea and the traffic and the birds for the plays on the wireless?' And Mrs Stone, who loved the wireless plays and found in them a small solace in her widowhood, answered truthfully: 'I've never thought about it, Micky, but I expect someone goes out with a machine and collects them. I expect a man does.' And Micky nodded. 'I think I'll become that man,' he told her.

It was a job you travelled for. Your life was a scavenge-hunt. You had lists: abattoir, abbey, accordion, balloon ascent, barcarole, beaver and on and on through the alphabet of things living and wild and man-made that breathed or thumped or yodelled or burned or sang. It was a beautiful life, Micky thought. He pitied the millions who sat in rooms all their working days and had never heard a redshank or a bullfrog. Some people said to him, 'I bet it's a lonely life, just listening to things, Micky?' But he didn't agree and he thought it presumptuous of people to suggest this. The things he liked listening to least were words.

Yet Micky Stone had a kind of loneliness in him, a small one, growing bigger as he aged. It was connected to the feeling that there had been a better time than now, a short but perfect time, in fact, and that nothing in his life, not even his liking of his work, would ever match it. He remembers this now, as the sky above the field becomes heavy and dark with the snow yet to fall: the time of Harriet Cavanagh, he calls it, or in other words, the heyday.

Suffolk is a rich place for sound. Already, in four days, Micky Stone has collected half an hour of different winter birds. His scavenge list includes a working windmill, a small town market, a livestock auction and five minutes of sea. He's staying at a bed-and-breakfast in a small town not far from the cottage with the metal windows where he heard his first sounds. He's pleased to be near this place. Though the houses are smarter and the landscape emptier now, the familiar names on the signposts and the big openness of the sky give him a sense of things unaltered. It's not difficult, here, to remember the shy, secretive man he was at nineteen and to recreate in the narrow lanes the awesome sight of Harriet Cavanagh's ramrod back and neat beige bottom sitting on her pony. The thing he loved most about this girl was her deportment. He was a slouch, his mother often told him, a huddler. Harriet Cavanagh was as perfectly straight as a bamboo. And flying like a pennant from her head was her long, straight hair, the colour of cane. Micky Stone would crouch by the gate at the end of his mother's garden, close his eyes and wait for the first sound of the horse. It always trotted, never walked. Harriet Cavanagh was a person in a hurry, flying into her future. Then, as the clip-clop of the hooves told Micky that the vision was in sight, he'd open his eyes and lift his head and Harriet in her haste would hail him with her riding crop, 'Hi, Micky!' and pass on. She'd be out of sight very quickly, but Micky would stand and listen till the sound of the trotting pony had completely died away. When he told his mother that he was going to marry Harriet Cavanagh, she'd sniffed and said unkindly, 'oh yes? And Princess Margaret Rose too, I dare say?' imagining that with these words she'd closed the matter. But the matter of Harriet Cavanagh didn't close. Ever. At fifty, with the winter lying silently about him, Micky Stone knows that it never will. As he packs his microphone away, the snow is falling densely and he hears himself hope that it will smother the fields and block the lanes and wall him up in its whiteness with his fabulous memories.

The next morning, as he brushes the snow from the windscreen of his car, he notices that the driver's side window has already been cleared of it – deliberately cleared, he imagines – as if someone had been peering in. Unlocking the door, he looks around at the quiet street of red Edwardian houses with white-painted gables on which the sun is now shining. It's empty of people, but the pavement is patterned with their footprints. They've passed and gone and it seems that one of them stopped and looked into Micky Stone's car.

He loads his equipment and drives out of the town. The roads are treacherous. He's looking forward to hearing the windmill when, a few miles out of the town, it occurs to Micky that this is one of the stillest days he can remember. Not so much as a breath of wind to turn the sails. He slows the car and thinks. He slows it to a stop and winds down the window and listens. The fields and hedgerows are icy, silent, glittering. On a day like this, Harriet Cavanagh once exclaimed as she passed the cottage gate, 'Gosh, it's beautiful, isn't it, Micky?' and the bit in the pony's mouth jingled as he sneezed and Micky noticed that the animal's coat was long and wondered if the winter would be hard.

Now he wonders what has become of the exact place by the hawthorn hedge where he used to stand and wait for Harriet on her morning rides. His mother is long dead, but he suspects that the cottage will be there, the windows replaced, perhaps, the boring garden redesigned. So he decides, while waiting for an east wind, to drive to the cottage and ask its owners whether they would mind if he did a wildtrack of their lane.

It's not far. He remembers the way. Through the smart little village of Pensford Green where now, he notices, the line of brick cottages are painted loud, childish colours and only the snow on their roofs unifies them as a rural terrace, then past two fields of apple trees, and there's the lane. What he can't remember now as he approaches it is whether the lane belonged to the house. Certainly, in the time when he lived there no cars ever seemed to come up it, only the farmers sometimes and in autumn the apple pickers and Harriet Cavanagh of course, who seemed, from her lofty seat in the saddle, to own the whole county.

Micky Stone feels nervous as the lane unfolds. The little car slithers. The lane's much longer than he remembers and steeper. The car, lurching up hill, nudges the banks, slews round and stops. Micky restarts the engine, then hears the wheels spin, making deep grooves in the snow. He gets out, looking for something to put under the wheels. The snow's almost knee-deep and there are no tracks in it except those his car has made. Micky wonders if the present tenants of the cottage sense that they're marooned.

Then it occurs to him that he has the perfect excuse for visiting them: 'I took a wrong turning and my car's stuck. I wondered whether you could help me?' Then, while they fetch sacks and a shovel from the old black shed, he'll stand waiting by the gate, his feet planted on the exact spot which, thirty years ago, he thought of as hallowed ground.

So he puts on his boots and starts out on foot, deciding not to take his machine. The silence of the morning is astonishing. He passes a holly tree that he remembers. Its berries this year are abundant. His mother, tall above her slouch-back of a son, used to steal branches from this tree to lay along her Christmas mantelpiece.

The tree wasn't far from the cottage. As he rounds the next bend, Micky expects to see it: the gate, the hawthorn hedge, the graceless little house with its low door. Yet it isn't where he thought it would be. He stops and looks behind him, trying to remember how far they used to walk, carrying the holly boughs. Then he stands still and listens. Often the near presence of a house can be heard: a dog barking, the squeak of a child's swing. But there's nothing at all.

Micky walks on. On his right, soon, he sees a break in the hedge. He hurries the last paces to it and finds himself looking into an empty field. The field slopes away from the hedge, just as the garden used to slope away. Micky walks forward, sensing that there's grass, not plough under his feet and he knows that the house was here. It never belonged to them, of course. When his mother left, it returned to the farmer from whom she'd rented it for twelve years. She'd heard it was standing empty. It was before the time of the scramble for property. No one had thought of it as a thing of value.

Micky stands for a while where the gate used to be. On my mark, he thinks. Yet the altered landscape behind him robs it of familiarity. It's as if, in removing the house, someone has removed his younger self from the place where he used to stand.

No point in staying, he decides, so he walks slowly back past the holly tree to his car. He gets in, releases the handbrake and lets it slip gently backwards down its own tracks. At the bottom of the lane, he starts the engine, reverses out into the road and drives away.

In the afternoon, he goes down to the shingly beach. The sun's low and the wind coming off the sea strong enough to make the sleeves of his anorak flap. He crouches near a breakwater. He sets up his machine, tests for sound levels, then holds the microphone at the ocean. He remembers his instructions: 'With the sea recording, Micky, try to get gulls and any other seabirds. And do plenty of selection, strong breakers close up, smaller splashing waves without much wind, and so on. Use your judgment.'

The scene his microphone is gathering is very beautiful. He wishes, for once, that he was gathering pictures as well as sound. The snow still lying high up on the beach and along the sea wall is almost violet-coloured in the descending afternoon. A film maker might wait months to capture this extraordinary light. Micky closes his eyes, forcing himself to concentrate on the sound only. When he opens them again, he sees a man standing still about thirty yards from him and staring at him.

Micky stays motionless, closes his eyes again, hears to his satisfaction gulls calling far off. When he opens his eyes once more, he sees that the man has come nearer, but is standing in the same attitude, intently watching Micky.

So Micky's thoughts return to the morning, to his discovery that someone had been peering into his car, then to his visit to the house which had gone, and he feels, not fear exactly, nor even suspicion, but a kind of troubled excitement and all the questions his mind has been asking for years about this place and the person he loved in it suddenly clamour in him for answers. He looks up at the stranger. He's a tall, straight-standing person. His hands are in the pockets of a long coat. In his stern look and in his straightness, he reminds Micky of Harriet Cavanagh's father, in the presence of whom Micky Stone felt acutely his own lack of height and the rounded disposition of his shoulders. But he tells himself that the fierce Major Cavanagh must now be an old man and this stranger is no more than forty-five, about the age Harriet herself would be.

Micky looks at his watch. He decides he will record three more minutes of sea and that then he will go over to the man and say what he now believes he's come here to do: 'I'm looking for Harriet Cavanagh. This may sound stupid. Are you in a position to help me?'

Then Micky turns away and tries to concentrate on the waves and the birds. He dreads speaking to the man because he was never any good at expressing himself. When Harriet Cavanagh said of the shiny white morning,

'Gosh, it's beautiful!' Micky was struck by her phrase like a whip and was speechless. Harriet had chosen a language that suited her: it was straight and direct and loud. Micky, huddled by his gate, knew that the dumbness of his first ten years had somehow lingered in his brain.

The three minutes seem long. The gulls circle and fight. Micky forces himself not to move a muscle. The sea breaks and is pulled back, rattling the shingle like coins, and breaks again. When Micky at last turns round, the man has gone.

On the edge of sleep, Micky hears the wind get up. Tomorrow, he will go to the windmill. He thinks, tonight I can hear my own loneliness like something inside me, turning.

Micky climbs up a broad ladder into the lower section of the mill. Its owner is a narrow-shouldered, rather frail seeming man who seems excited and pleased to show Micky round.

'It's funny,' says the skinny man as he opens the trap door to the big working chamber, 'my Dad once thought of buying a windmill, but he wanted to chuck out all the machinery and turn the thing into a house. But I'd never do that. I think far too many of the old, useful things have vanished.'

Micky nods and they mount a shorter ladder and scramble through the trap into the ancient body of the mill. Light comes from a window below the ratchet wheel and from the pulley hatch, where the sacks of corn are wound up and the bags of milled flour lowered.

'We're only in use for part of the year,' says the owner, 'but we can lower the grinding wheel so that you can get the sound of it.'

Micky nods and walks to the window and looks down. Every few moments his view of the icy fields is slashed by the passing of one of the sails, but he likes the feeling of being high up for once, not crouching or hiding. And as he stares and the arms of the windmill pass and re-pass, he thinks, I must stand up tall now for what I want and what I have always wanted and still do not possess: the sound of Harriet Cavanagh's voice.

'All right, then?' asks the mill owner, disappointed by Micky's silence. 'I'll set the wheel, shall I?'

Micky turns, startled. 'Thank you,' he says. 'I'll set up in here. Then I'll do a few minutes outside.'

'Good,' says the mill owner, then adds, 'I like the radio plays. "The Theatre of the Mind" someone said it was called and I think that's a good description because the mind only needs sound to imagine entire places, entire situations. Isn't that right?'

'Well,' says Micky, 'yes, I think it is.'

It's dark by the time Micky gets back to his lodgings. As he goes in, he can smell the meal his landlady is preparing, but he doesn't feel hungry, he's too anxious about what he's going to do. He's going to telephone the big house where Harriet lived until she married and went to live in the West Country. Though Major Cavanagh and his wife will be old, Micky senses that people who live comfortably live long and he feels certain that when the receiver is picked up it will be one of them who answers. And he knows exactly what he will say, he's prepared it. 'You won't remember me, Major, but I'm an old friend of Harriet's and would very much like to get in touch . . .'

There's a payphone near the draughty front door of the guest house. Micky arranges 10p coins in a pile on top of it and searches in the local directory for the number. It's there as he expected. Cavanagh, Major C.N.H., High House, Matchford.

He takes a deep breath. His landlady has a television in her kitchen and music and laughter from a comedy show are blaring out. Micky presses the receiver tight to his ear and tries to shut out the noise. He dials the number. He hears it ring six times before it's picked up and a voice he remembers as Mrs Cavanagh's says graciously, 'Matchford two one five.'

'Mrs Cavanagh,' Micky begins, after pressing in the first of the coins, 'you won't remember me, but –'

'This isn't Mrs Cavanagh.' says the voice, 'Will you hold on and I'll get her.'

102

'Harriet?' says Micky.

There's a pause. Micky reaches out and holds on tightly to the top of the payphone box.

'Yes. Who is this?'

'Micky Stone.'

Another pause. The laughter from the landlady's TV is raucous.

'Sorry. Who?'

'Micky Stone. You probably won't remember me. I used to live with my mother in Slate Cottage.'

'Oh yes. I remember you. Micky Stone. Gosh.'

'I didn't think you'd be here, Harriet. I was going to ask where you were so that I could ring you up and talk to you.'

'Were you? Heavens. What about?'

Another burst of laughter comes out of the kitchen. Micky covers his left ear with his hand. 'I hadn't planned what about. About the old days, or something. About your pony.'

'Golly yes. I remember. You used to stand at the gate . . .'

'Wait!' says Micky. 'Can you wait a moment? Can you hang on?'

'Yes. All right. Why?'

'Hang on, please, Harriet. I'll only be a minute.'

Micky feeds another 10p coin into the pay slot, then runs as fast as he can up the stairs to his room. He grabs the tape machine and the microphone and hurtles down again. His landlady opens her kitchen door and stares as he rushes past. He picks up the telephone. The recorder is on and turning, the little mike held against Micky's head.

'Harriet? Are you still there?'

A pause. Micky hears the door of the kitchen close.

'Yes.'

'So you remember me at the gate?'

'Yes . . .'

'I once helped whitewash your stables and the dairy . . .'

'Yes. Lucky.'

'What?'

'Lucky. My little horse. He was called Lucky. My children have got ponies now, but they don't awfully care about them. Not like I cared about Lucky.'

'You rode so well.'

'Did I? Yes. I loved that, the early morning rides. Getting up in the dark. It was quite a long way to your lane. I think it'd usually be light, wouldn't it, by the time I came up there? And I'd be boiling by that time, even in snowy weather. Terribly hot, but awfully happy. And I remember, if you weren't there sometimes, if you were working or having breakfast or something, I used to think it was rather a bad omen. I was so superstitious, I used to think the day would go badly or Lucky would throw me, or Mummy would be cross or something, and quite often it went like that – things did go wrong if I hadn't seen you. Isn't that stupid? I'd forgotten all that till I spoke to you, but that's exactly how it was. I suppose you could say you were my good luck charm. And actually, I've often thought about you and wondered how you'd got on. I was rather sad when they demolished Slate Cottage. Did you know they had? I remember thinking every bit of one's life has kind of *landmarks* and Slate Cottage was definitely a landmark for me and I don't like it that it's not there any more. But you knew it had gone, did you?'

'Not till today . . .'

'Oh, it went years ago. Like lots of things. Like Lucky and the morning rides. Horrid, I think. I hate it when things are over. My marriage is over. That's why I'm staying here. So sad and horrid it's all been. It just makes me think – jolly stupidly, because I know one can never bring time back – but it does make me see that those days when I was growing up and you were my lucky charm were important. What I mean is, they were good.'

Lying in bed, Micky waits till the house is quiet. Outside his window, the snow is falling again. When he switches on the recorder and listens to Harriet's voice, he realises for the first time that he forgot to put in a new tape and that most of his work at the windmill is now obliterated. About a minute of it remains, however. As Harriet Cavanagh fades to silence, her words are replaced by the sound of the big sails going round and round.

The Kite Flyer

In my captors' glossless eyes do I see an enviousness of the lustre in mine own.

– from the Prison Treatise of Anna of Didsmill 1643

VERY OFTEN, WHEN Olivia Kingswell spoke encouragingly or chidingly to herself, she addressed herself as 'my dear'. 'Pick up the pieces, my dear.' 'Don't make a spectacle of yourself, my dear.'

Then, on a certain day, a Sunday in early summer, she decided to break this habit. 'You are Olivia,' she told her bulgy blue eyes in the hall mirror, 'it's as simple as that.' And she felt amazed, as she went to the kitchen to baste the Sunday joint, that she'd been so polite, so over-polite to herself for so long. 'It's ridiculous!' she sniffed.

On the same Sunday, her husband, Anthony Kingswell, as he sat and waited for his beef and potatoes, felt cold. The coal scuttle in the sitting room was empty. He took it out to the coal bunker and filled it up, fetched dry kindling from the woodshed and made a fire. It was May. The light coming in to the Kingswells' sitting room was so glaring that the colours of Anthony's fire looked feeble. He knelt over it, holding out his hands.

Olivia, her apron on, her nose pink from the hot kitchen, came in. She had the carriage of a Great Dane, Anthony thought, stately but bounding. Today, on his knees, he felt small beside his wife.

'Darling,' she said, 'what are you doing?'

'Trying to warm up,' he said.

'It's *May*,' said Olivia.

'I know it's May,' said Anthony.

Sunday was usually the day when Anthony Kingswell felt warmest, happiest and most close to God.

For nine years, as Vicar of the Church of St Barnabas, Didsmill, he had thought of Sunday as 'belonging' to him. This wasn't arrogance, it was simply a reaffirmation, as the Church years succeeded one another, that he had chosen the right profession. Walking, in early light, from the vicarage gate to the vestry door, smelling damp yew, touching the iron cold of the latch, he would feel God slumbering in his blood. Then, robing for Communion, as old Tom Willis tugged out with leathery hands a funereal clang from the bell, his cheeks would start to become rosy with Jesus, his fingernails pink and shiny with Jesus, and at his throat would wait the syllables of praise and thanksgiving for the knowledge that God was now wide awake in his body. Even in the depths of winter, Anthony was warm on Sundays. He could have given January sermons in his underwear. He'd look out at his meagre congregation, hunched up in overcoats and scarves and woolly hats and think, Poor things, I hold up the chalice to their lips and they sip, and yet they're chilly. What a sad coldness this must be.

Now, on this Sunday in May, the second Sunday before Whitsun, here was Anthony lighting a fire and kneeling in front of it and shivering. He knew it had been growing in him for some weeks, this awful feeling of being cold. In the same way, Olivia's awareness that she had been too polite, too evasive a person had been growing in her for about the same number of weeks, though neither Olivia nor Anthony could have said for precisely how long. However, these things were happening: God was slipping out of Anthony's veins, Olivia had learned the rightness, the sternness and the beauty, even, of her Christian name.

Though she was a conscientious vicar's wife – efficient at fund-raising, gentle-voiced, an enthusiastic maker of

110

bramble jelly – Olivia had never been very curious about faith. She saw it as something Anthony possessed and always would, and which she didn't and never would, like a penis. It neither worried her, nor made her envious. What she had acknowledged – until recently, until she made one of the great discoveries of her life – was that her life lacked purpose. She would sit at Matins and watch her husband mount his pulpit, and know that Anthony and the Church of England were like the desert traveller and his camel, self-sufficient in the midst of emptiness, going patiently on from one small oasis to another. Olivia never yearned for her own camel. She got on with the years. One of the things she loved most about life was discovering the past. She often felt that without her local library she would have been a rather morose woman, but history made her excitable. And then, quite by chance, among the red and green and brown spines of the seventeenth century, she discovered Anna of Didsmill Wold.

One of the questions never asked by those later involved in the 'case' of Anthony and Olivia Kingswell was 'Why did Anna of Didsmill inspire Olivia in the way she did?' The answer (or at least *part* of the answer) lay in the fact that Anna was not only a martyr to her cause and a woman of action, she was also the eldest daughter of a country schoolmaster (as was Olivia), she was born on July 16th, 1620 (exactly three hundred and fourteen years to the day before Olivia), and is known, in prison, to have asked her captors for a dish of greengages, Olivia's favourite fruit. Thus, it was immediately clear to Olivia that she shared much 'common ground' with Anna. Part of this 'common ground' was the actual earth on which they both walked – the lanes, the fields and the wold of Didsmill. As Olivia's hands turned the pages of Anna's history, they trembled.

To summarise for those who do not know of her, Anna of Didsmill was born into a moderately poor Puritan family five years before the accession of Charles I. At the age of twenty-two, shepherding her father's flock of pupils into the school yard one August morning in 1642, Anna heard the voice of her stern God coming out of the school-house

111

weathercock. The voice told her to emulate the Maid of Orleans, to don a soldier's uniform and help bring victory to the Protestant cause against the King.

That same night, wearing her brother's clothes, she rode secretly to Fenny Stratford, where Cromwell was camped, and two months later she was fighting with his army at Edge Hill. During the battle, she fell from her horse and was captured by the Royalists. In prison, her identity as a woman was quickly revealed. She was abused by her guards, raped and tortured. She was tried for treason, found guilty and hung at Didsmill gibbet. While in prison, she wrote (and smuggled out) a treatise on the wrongs she had suffered at the hands of men, exemplifying all the evils and degradations society metes out to women. Thus, she was both a woman of action and a reformer. Yet historians had neglected her. She languished in Olivia's library in one small book. Olivia rescued her. She gave a talk to the Didsmill and Didsborn W.I. about her. She discovered the cottage where she'd lived and the site of the old schoolhouse (burned down in 1805) where she heard God's voice. Slowly, yet persuasively, Anna was entering Olivia's mind. And one day, Olivia walked on the downland where the gibbet had once stood. She knew there would be no trace of it. On the exact spot where Anna of Didsmill had died, there was an aircraft hanger and the land for six miles around it was a criss-cross of runways and concrete barracks. It was an American airbase. It was rumoured that missile silos were going to be built here.

Olivia put her hands up to the perimeter fence and imagined that this woman of long ago spoke to her in the sighing of the wire: 'Do what you can,' the voice said kindly.

If it was quite easy, then, to understand why Olivia Kingswell found a new direction of her life through her discovery of Anna of Didsmill Wold, it was much more difficult to determine (and remember, these two events went on simultaneously) why Anthony Kingswell began to lose his faith.

On this May Sunday, when he lit his feeble fire, Anthony was fifty-four years old and had held his faith in a forgiving and accessible God for more than twenty years. He had entered the Church at the age of thirty-three, the age of Christ's death. (He liked the events of his life to reverberate.) He had never regretted it. He had always imagined his faith would last him out. God was tangible to Anthony. When he snuffled on his pipe, he felt God in the embers and in his saliva. When he dreamed about his boyhood, he saw God in that space of bony flesh between the hem of his flannel shorts and the turnover of his grey socks.

You might suggest that, because he was a man who felt God to be so much a part of the physical world, he was bound to feel the presence of God diminishing as his middle age advanced. Though a good preacher, he wasn't a truly spiritual man. His faith was instinctive, not cerebral. And this fact seemed, in part, to explain what was happening. For some reason, his mind, his rational self had started to question, or at least to worry about, the existence of God. Being the man he was, he sought to reassure himself by finding God in His usual places – in his pipe embers, in the dry, sweet smell of the altar rail, in the vicarage garden, and most of all in his own blood. So, when he found that he felt cold, it was natural that he also felt afraid.

The vicarage, where Anthony and Olivia had lived for nine years, was a solid, Victorian, well-ordered house. Olivia managed it well, yet inhabited it lightly, keeping a careful distance from Anthony's study, which, as visiting parishoners usually sensed, was the only 'serious' room in the house. It had never been suggested that Olivia might occupy a 'serious' room of her own. 'For what?' Anthony would have asked. 'To write the W.I. Newsletter in?'

But then, after Olivia had discovered Anna, she began to have a recurring dream in which she walked aimlessly through her house, topping up the flower water, polishing coasters, plumping cushions, readying each room for

113

someone else, always for someone else, till her own presence in the house became as faded as chintz and the rooms were like lazy strangers, just sitting about, offering nothing. So she turned a guest room into her 'serious' room. She removed the bed. She bought a cheap desk, a filing cabinet and a worklamp. Bookshelves were put up. She took down the chintz at the window. She put *A Life of Anna of Didsmill*, alone as yet, in place on the new bookshelves.

Anthony came and stared at these changes and stared at Olivia and pulled his cardigan closer round his body.

'What's it all for?' he asked.

'My work,' she said lightly.

'You've got no curtains, Olivia,' was his only comment.

Her 'work' progressed faster than she'd imagined. Making constant trips to her library and inspirational demands upon the chief librarian's time, she discovered numerous references to Anna in detailed histories of the Civil War. One of these books mentioned that Anna's prison Treatise (or what remained of it) was kept in the Bodleian Library. Two days after learning this, Olivia was in Oxford, holding twenty-three yellowed and stained pages of Anna's words in her hands. She felt, as they were unlocked from a glass case and handed to her, as if she was about to faint. She sat down and ate a peppermint. A research assistant brought her a magnifying glass.

It was early June now. While Olivia was away, Anthony wrote to his friend, Canon Stapleton in Winchester, whose footsteps into the Church he'd once followed. 'I feel,' he said in the letter, 'as if the great bird that is the Trinity, its warm body and its two protecting wings have flown away and left me.' He thought that writing these words to Canon Stapleton might comfort him, but it didn't. He got up from his writing desk and walked, his face set hard, up to Olivia's study. He stood at the door. One shelf was almost filled with books now. Anthony stared and stared. His wife's endeavours filled him with dread. He wanted to scrumple up the papers that now littered the desk and hurl them out of the window into the June wind.

Unluckily for Anthony, this particular summer was cool. Sunlight on the garden, particularly sunlight on the grey-green poplar leaves, shivering, flashing, he imagined as 'God's currency'. He loved to sit in a comfortable chair, his eyes two thin slits just open on this glory. But, in June, there didn't seem to be many glorious days. The sky was moody. Anthony looked up at the sunless blanket and said, 'Why, oh my Redeemer, have you hidden your coinage from your servant?' Then he glanced at the window of Olivia's study, wide open. She worked on, oblivious of weather. She had a title for an article, she told Anthony: *Anna of Didsmill, A Heroine for Today*. If the article was published, she would try to gather enough material for a book. When she talked about these things, her bulgy eyes were wide, like a child's eyes open on her first sight of the sea. And Anthony shuddered. How well he recognised that shining light. He had grown used to finding it, many times a week, in his own face in the mirror. '*I* used to be the one!' he wanted to say to his wife. 'I should be the one!'

It was Monday. Anthony walked in from the garden. On Monday evenings Anthony always held a 'surgery' for his parishoners. Today, the thought of the surgery appalled him. He needed to receive advice, not give it.

He poured himself a glass of sherry and sat down in the sitting room. He held his glass up to the light, and stared at the liquid. One of his most secret ways of finding God was in sherry. He lit his pipe, warming his hands on the bowl. The warm pipe, the cold, strong sherry, he calmed himself with these, filling and refilling his glass and muttering peculiar prayers as, upstairs, Olivia worked on.

Not long after this Monday (Anthony had been too ill with his sherry drinking to hold his surgery and the people who came talked to Olivia instead), Olivia declared that Anna had 'instructed' her to make a trip to Greenham Common.

115

Anthony stared at his wife.

'No, Olivia,' he said.

She stared back at him. Colossal she seemed. A warrior. She's becoming a man, Anthony thought.

'I'm sorry, Anthony darling,' she said, 'I'm just *telling* you that I am going to Greenham on my birthday, July 16th. I am not asking for permission.'

'I can't have it,' said Anthony, 'a vicar's wife simply must not take part in this kind of political antic.'

'It's not an antic,' said Olivia, 'and anyway, churchmen and politicians are more closely linked over the question of peace than over any other, as you yourself should be aware.'

And she strode out of the kitchen where they had been eating supper and bounded upstairs to her study. Anthony heard the key turn in the lock, got up from the table, went to the Welsh dresser which, since Olivia's mother's death in 1971, had proudly displayed a Wedgewood dinner service, took down five plates and a gravy boat and smashed them on the stone floor. Olivia did not come down. He took up two more plates and hurled them at the chimneybreast. Olivia unlocked her door, ran down the stairs and into the kitchen and hit her husband in the face. He sat down among the broken china and started to cry. Olivia stared at him, disgusted. Children! she thought scornfully. Men are *children*! But then, he reached out for her hands and held them to his face. 'Help me, Olivia,' he sobbed. 'I'm losing Jesus.'

Olivia postponed the trip to Greenham. Instead, Canon Stapleton (whose reply to Anthony's Trinity letter had been vague and dismissive) was persuaded by Olivia to come and stay with them. The weather brightened in July, and Anthony and Canon Stapleton went for long walks in the Didsmill beechwoods. 'Something,' said Stapleton to Anthony, 'has made you angry with God. That's all. You're angry with Him and through your anger you've lost Him. If you can remember *why* you're angry with Him, then you'll be able to forgive Him and beg His forgiveness and you will find him again. Tiffs with God are more normal than you imagine.'

On they walked, under the green fanlights of beech, and Anthony listened and felt hope revive. But, search as he tried, he simply couldn't remember why he was angry with God. He knew why he was angry with Olivia, but he couldn't remember why he was angry with God, or even if he *was* angry, and after some days, Canon Stapleton had to return to Winchester and at his departure Anthony felt invaded by despair.

That same day, Olivia's outline for her article was accepted by *History in Perspective*, a monthly history magazine. As Olivia showed Anthony the letter, her eyes were luminous with joy. He stared morosely past her, so envious of her happiness he couldn't utter. She smiled. She crowed. 'I'm determined there'll be a book,' she said.

'Beware of pride,' he muttered and handed her back the letter. A look of disbelief crossed her face. 'Anthony,' she said breathlessly, 'this quarrel of yours with God, please don't turn it into a quarrel with me!'

You might say that the events described so far represented the 'first stage' in the odd case of Anthony and Olivia Kingswell. From this point, they entered the 'second stage' or 'second act', if you like, of what some would later describe as a tragedy.

The second stage really began that night when, lying in the dark beside his wife, Anthony Kingswell stumbled on the notion that it was Olivia who was responsible for God's withdrawal from him, that it was Olivia who, by seeking to change the natural order of things with her wretched Martyr of Didsmill, was deflecting God away from him and towards herself.

This was a strangely irrational decision for Anthony to come to. No one knew better than Anthony that Olivia's faith was, at best, peripheral to her life. She'd always been happy to let him be the believer and had certainly never shown any sign of wanting to get closer to God than she already was. This, however, Anthony decided as he lay and looked at his wife's sleeping body, must have been a deliberate deception. She must have been envious of his faith for years and waited, waited for her chance to deflect it . . .

Without waking Olivia, Anthony got out of bed and went down to his study. Outside the window, he could hear the cry of a nightingale and he felt more at peace, more assuaged than he'd felt for months. He reached for his bible and turned to the *Epistle of Paul to the Ephesians*, Chapter 5, verse 24: . . . *as the Church is subject unto Christ, so let the wives be to their husbands in every thing.*

Then, in his neat and rather beautiful writing, he wrote out these words on a card, tiptoed to the kitchen and propped the card up on the Welsh dresser in the exact place where the gravy boat used to stand. He breathed deeply. He could sense, through the Venetian blind, the approach of dawn and he knelt and prayed: 'In the coming of morning let me feel you again, my true and only God. Like a lover who runs to the shore as the sails of his beloved are glimpsed on the horizon, let me run to meet you in the sunrise and find you there.' He stayed in his attitude of prayer, with his chin on the kitchen table, till he could feel the room fill with soft, yellowy light. Olivia, in her dressing-gown, found him like this and touched his head gently. 'Come back to bed, Anthony. It's only half past five,' she said. And he opened his eyes. It seemed to him that in the split second before Olivia touched him, he had felt it near him, waiting, the Holy Spirit. In another moment, as the kitchen filled with the dawn, it would have entered him.

'You prevented it!' he cried, and turned upwards to his wife a face of stone.

Not long after this, Olivia went to Greenham.

Courage in the midst of desolation had always moved her. She had remembered all her life a story her schoolmaster father had told her about a tribe of American Indians called the Ram Tiku, whose sacred valley had been destroyed by lumberjacks. Generations of these Indians, living now on dry, difficult earth, sent their braves in to reclaim the valley, until there were no young men left and the valley became a shrine in the mind, not a place anyone could remember. The perseverance of the Greenham women reminded Olivia of the perseverance of the Ram Tiku. The American soldiers had the tough, beefy faces of lumberjacks. The women's 'benders' were like polythene tepees. And life – such as it could be there – congregated round little fires. Drinking Bovril, Olivia told a group of young women (some of their faces were like the painted faces of braves) the story of Anna of Didsmill. They listened eagerly. 'Didsmill,' said a stern-browed woman called Josie, 'we must start thinking about Didsmill. Next year they're building silos there.'

The group round Olivia grew. Someone gave her a helping of bean stew on a plastic plate.

'You know,' said Olivia, 'if Anna had been on the side of the King, as Joan of Arc was on the side of her King, she would have become a heroine, a saint perhaps. It's what side you're on that matters. I've understood this now.'

There was rueful laughter. Olivia looked round at the squatting women spooning up their stew. 'Forgive me,' she wanted to say to them. 'Forgive me my sheltered life. It's going to change.'

'I would really like,' she said at length, looking round at the camp, with its mud and its urban litter, 'to help begin something at Didsmill. I think it's going to become an important place.'

It was a warm but windy day. On the Didsmill down-land the wind was fierce as Anthony came out of the vicarage, hurled his home-made kite into the car and drove fast to the rolling hills above the Didsmill base.

Here, he got out and threw his head back and imagined, under the white bellies of the clouds, the earth turning. He felt a sudden lightness. His spirits lifted. He gathered up his kite and started to run with it, playing the string out behind him. It was an insubstantial thing and it began to lift almost at once. Anthony stopped running and held the taut line. He'd made kites since he was a boy, dragon kites, aeroplane kites, seagull kites. He knew how to handle them. And today's wind was perfect. The kite was white and he watched it turn and dance, turn and dance, then stream off higher, tearing at the string. He ran with it again. It was almost at the limit of the strong nylon line now and Anthony felt weightless, so full of the spirit of the kite he almost believed he could follow it aloft, up and up into the fathomless blue . . . And then he saw what he hoped would happen: half a mile above him, the kite began to break up. The white paper sheets were torn from the fragile frame and came flying down to earth like a scatter of leaves. Anthony watched them fall, the twenty-three white pages of Olivia's article, he watched them scatter and tear and go flying off over the curves of the hill. The kite string was limp in his hand and he was breathing hard. 'Beautiful . . .' he murmured. And he knelt.

So she returned from Greenham to find her article (of which she had made no duplicate) gone.

'Where is it, Anthony?' she said, patiently.

'On the downs,' he said from the depths of his pillows.

Returning from the kite flying, he had lain down exhausted on his bed and slept, and when he woke the exhaustion was still there and he slept again, and now he felt entombed in the bed and couldn't move. He was pale and his eyes were hectic. He's going mad, Olivia thought.

He lay and stared at his room. He thought of autumn coming and then winter and he knew that his soul was filling up with ice. But it was clear to him now: the light he saw in Olivia's eyes was *his* light. She had stolen it. It was God's light and it belonged to him. Without it, he would grow colder and colder. On the windy down, destroying her article, he had stolen some of it back. For a few moments, it had warmed him. But it hadn't lasted. And here was Olivia, strong as a stag beside his bed.

'I'll write it again, you know.' she said through hard, set lips and she turned and bounded from the room. His door slammed. She was without sympathy for him.

He didn't speak to her for two days and she didn't speak

to him. He stayed in bed. She worked in her room. She fed him frozen pies and jelly on smeared trays she hadn't bothered to wipe. On the third day, he left her. Weak and grey, he put a small suitcase in the car and drove to Winchester, where Canon Stapleton took him in. 'All I can advise,' said Canon Stapleton, 'is some time in retreat.'

So Anthony entered Muir Priory. He was given a tiny, white room with a narrow, uncurtained window. On one of the walls was an ivory crucifix.

The second draft of Olivia's article was completed in ten days and she knew it was better than the first.

September came, dry, windy and bright. Olivia typed out the article (careful, this time, to keep a copy of it) and sent it off to *History in Perspective* and waited. While waiting, she wrote to the Greenham woman, Josie, and asked if she would come and stay with her, 'to make concrete plans for something at Didsmill'.

When she thought about Anthony, she felt cross with God. He could be so spiteful, this supposedly loving Deity. It was mean of Him to have withdrawn from Anthony's spittle. But she was aware that, among these thoughts, crouched her knowledge of her own withdrawal from her husband. He had always preferred God to her and she'd always accepted this. God was, as she'd so often imagined during Matins, Anthony's camel; she was simply the mat, frayed by desert winds, on which the rider had lain. Now, she was tired of being a mat and she folded it away. The camel lay buried in an eternity of sand. The rider was hungry, lost. The nights were cold. Olivia felt wistful, yet unmoved. She tore the card on the dresser into pieces, made up her bed with clean sheets that held no trace of the smell of Anthony. Let the men heal each other, she thought.

The vicarage, without Anthony, was very quiet. Olivia filled it with bowls of greengages and with whispered conversations to Anna. 'Anna,' she said, making sandwiches for the visit of the temporary vicar, 'I am fifty-one.'

The temporary vicar was a fat, pasty man. 'I suffer from acidity,' he said as he ate Olivia's tea.

'You know,' Olivia heard herself reply, 'I don't think I'm interested in symptoms any more, only in causes.'

The vicar belched and smiled. 'Well,' he said, wiping his mouth with his napkin, 'fishpaste is one.'

When he left, Olivia knew how glad she was to be alone. She got out the Ordnance Survey map and calculated the distance from Greenham to Didsmill. It was twenty-three miles. Anna was twenty-three when she was hung. Twenty-three pages of her treatise remained. While in prison, she wrote to her mother and father twenty-three times, asking for forgiveness.

Then Josie arrived. She was very tired and dirty. Olivia, gentle as a mother, ran a deep bath for her in the big, old-fashioned bath, put her to bed and brought her supper on a clean tray.

In Muir Priory, away from his parish and its responsibilities, away from Olivia, Anthony began to feel calmer.

Dean Neville Scales, warden of the Priory, was a long-limbed man with a passion for gardening. He liked to preach about God in Nature. He made sure that the Priory gardens were colourful and neat, his pride and joy being a grove of Japanese acers, scarlet and gold and purple.

The first leaves were going from the acers as Anthony walked alone on the priory lawns. Dew on the springy grass: God's moisture everywhere except on his own tongue. He wetted and wetted his lips. Prayer came to him lightly, its syllables flowing freely into his mind. This was a benevolent sign. He walked and prayed and, though the contours of the garden were mirror-sharp, he felt on his forehead some warmth from the sun.

He liked the simple, stark routine of each day and he liked the emptiness of his room. When he thought about his home, it seemed like a place too cluttered with objects and with feeling. He saw Olivia in it everywhere – Olivia's light. I hate her, he thought.

To Dean Scales he confessed. 'I still feel loving kindness

towards all things, or at least to most things, but not towards my wife.'

In the Dean's silence, he detected shock.

'God's ministers cannot harbour hatred,' he said, blowing his nose on a clean square of silk. 'Whatever your wife has done, you must try to forgive her.'

'I can't, Dean.'

'Are you telling me she's in mortal sin?'

'No, Dean.'

'Then your hatred is petty?'

Anthony sighed. He felt ashamed to say that his hate sprang from envy. The enviousness itself seemed, in the confessional, vain and silly, his idea that Olivia had 'stolen' God from him fanciful and stupid. He felt humble and sick. He longed, longed for some relief from his confusions.

'Let me stay here till I find God again, Dean.'

'We shall see how you progress.'

'I can't go back into the world.'

'And your responsibilities?'

'I can't honour them, till I find Jesus . . .'

'What makes you believe you will find Jesus here?'

Anthony sighed deeply. 'I must,' he said, 'or I shall go mad.'

Two weeks passed. The leaves on the gold acers were edged with brown. In everything, Anthony strove for obedience – from the cleaning of his supper plate (one evening, the Priory cook served up hamburgers and the raucous, treacherous world came teeming back into Anthony's head and made wounds in his fragile calm) to the hour-by-hour discomfort of kneeling. Each day was punctuated by fourteen 'stations of prayer', this punitive number echoing the fourteen Stations of the Cross. The first station was at five-thirty and the last at midnight. The time for sleep was short, but it was a grateful, dreamless sleep that Anthony slept. On the edge of it, in his curtainless room, he'd lie and look out at the stars and allow into his troubled head thoughts of heaven.

Josie Mecklin was a tanned, freckled woman with the patient smile of a teacher. During her stay in Olivia's house, she expected to instruct this middle-class vicar's wife on the true meaning of hardship and deprivation. But, to her surprise, she found she spent a lot of time listening to Olivia talking about martyrdom and belief. Olivia, it seemed, didn't need telling what had to be done. 'I think,' said this Great Dane, this stag of a woman, 'we are the "new Amazons". We're middle-aged, middle-class, pampered and ignorant. But we're *strong*. We're strong because we've understood. We'll fight to the death.'

Josie stayed three days. She spent a lot of time lying in the bath. She'd talk to Olivia through the bathroom door. A plan emerged from the clouds of steam: on the anniversary of the death of Anna of Didsmill, October 3rd, two hundred women would march from Greenham to the Didsmill base. They would take candles and brushwood torches. They would arrive at Didsmill as the sun went down and hold a silent, night-long vigil at the main gate. At first light Olivia would read aloud passages from Anna's treatise. Then they would disperse peacefully, many of them to walk the twenty-three miles back to Greenham.

Olivia, sitting on a hard chair in the passage, felt her heart begin to race. No moment in her life now seemed as meaningful as this one – her marriage, the birth of her two sons, Anthony's ordination, none of these milestones had knocked with such strength on her ribs. She put a hand to her chest. 'Let me not die, God, before these things happen.'

Pink and shiny from her baths, Josie ate hungrily in Olivia's kitchen. Over cups of coffee, maps came out and a route from Greenham to Didsmill was decided on. It was also decided that Olivia would return to Greenham with Josie and spend a riciprocal three days there, talking to the women about Anna and enlisting volunteers for the Didsmill march. In her loft, Olivia found a sleeping bag used by one of her sons at scout camp. It smelt of mothballs and it had a damp, cold feel. But already, Olivia could imagine her body inside it, warming it up.

On the morning of Olivia's departure with Josie, a letter arrived from *History in Perspective*. 'Thank you,' it said, 'for your interesting and excellently researched article. We would like to offer you the sum of £150 and we will hope to include the article in our February issue.'

Olivia drew Josie's hard shoulders towards her and let her excitement crackle in an impulsive kiss on her new friend's cheek.

On October 2nd, God returned to take up temporary lodging in Anthony's body.

He was in the Priory library, searching for a book Dean Scales had recommended to him, called *Nazareth and 20th Century Man*. A young curate, a withdrawn person Anthony had never spoken to, was sitting at one of the library tables. As Anthony passed him, he noticed that the curate was reading the very book Anthony had come into the library to find. Anthony stopped. He sat down opposite the curate and stared at the man's lowered head and at the book under his white hands. He felt like a supplicant. 'I have made,' he said in prayer and with a strange confusion of metaphor, 'my willow cabin at your gate, Lord. In it, I stand and wait. I serve you, but you do not come to me.' At this point in Anthony's prayer, the curate looked up at him and smiled and handed Anthony the book. The young man then got up without a word and walked out of the library. Anthony held the book to his chest. It was warm from the other man's touch. At last, at *last* a sign had been given. Tears came to his eyes. The tears were hot. With a sob of joy, he felt God streaming down his face.

Anthony left Muir Priory with the Dean's blessing on the late afternoon of the following day.

It seemed very strange to him to be driving his car. It was raining. His hands fumbled to find the windscreen wipers. The noise of the car distressed him. The houses he passed seemed ugly beyond imagining. He began to long for the beauty of his garden and the peace of his church.

He was full of anxiety. The world, he thought, opposes God's habitation in me. He drove on. In the cloudy sky, the light went early and the road in front of Anthony grew pale, its contours indistinct. But as darkness came on and blotted out the landscape around him, he felt calmer.

As he neared Didsmill, the rain ceased. Anthony stopped the car on a quiet road and got out, hoping, before the world and Olivia sprang at him again, to catch a glimpse of the same stars he'd seen from his window in the Priory. But the sky was uniform black and Anthony felt disappointment change to fear. He needed reassurance. He needed a *sign*. The stars, in place above him, would have been a sign.

He was about to get back into the car, when, far along the road in front of him, yet seeming to lie exactly in the path of the car, he saw a flickering light. It was a fluid, yellowy light, moving, beckoning. 'There it is,' Anthony whispered, 'my sign.'

And he began to walk towards it. As he neared it, he saw that the light was moving across the road, not towards him as he had believed. He squinted at it. It undulated under the trees. And now there was a faint sound accompanying the light, a shuffle of feet, and Anthony knew that, far from being alone on the road as he had thought, he was with a great shapeless, hidden gathering of people.

He could see them now: a slow procession, a long, long line of marchers holding candles and torches. He stood in the shadow of the trees, hiding. He could hear hundreds of voices, whispering, laughing. Women's voices. He turned away. The lights and the voices seemed to follow him, mocking. *You took us for a sign!* He tried to pray, but all his mind would construct were the four syllables of his wife's name: O-li-vi-a!

The threads were gathering now. The ending of the story of Anthony and Olivia Kingswell was coming . . .

All night, in the dusty, unkempt house he could barely recognise as his home, Anthony sat and waited for his wife. He grew cold. A wind got up. Anthony covered himself with a blanket. He dozed in the chair and dreamed of his future: his pulpit had been rebuilt in gold; it was higher than before. From it, he looked down on the potato faces of his parishoners. 'I,' he thundered, 'am the plough-man, and I plough you into the earth!' He woke shivering and trembling. He stared at the room, ghostly now in dawn light: dead flowers on the table, dust and crumbs on the carpet, old newspapers on the arms of chairs, boxes of leaflets piled up where a vase pedestal used to stand . . .

When she came in at last, the room was filled with sunlight and she wasn't alone. She stared at him. The woman at her back stared at him.

'Anthony,' she said coldly, 'why didn't you let me know you were coming back?' And she crossed the room and kissed him and he could feel her hard forehead against his, bruising him.

He said nothing. She pulled away and looked at him. So thin, he is, was her thought. 'This is Josie,' she said, and the woman smiled. Anthony pushed the blanket off his body and stood up. He was freezing.

'There's a fine wind, Olivia,' he said. 'Let's go for a walk together. We can take a kite.'

Sleep, thought Olivia. I have never wanted sleep so much as I want it now. But she agreed to go with him. Later, she would sleep.

As she went out with Anthony, she heard Josie upstairs, running a bath and Olivia knew that, tired as she was, she was at last happy in her life.

But the life of Olivia Kingswell had only minutes – twenty-three minutes exactly – to last.

Anthony didn't drive to the downs. He drove to a potato field, a large field spread round a deep pond, muddy and grim in its recent harvest, with a few rotting potatoes left among the cut stalks. Here, with his nylon kite string strong as wire, he strangled Olivia and threw her body into the pond. The body didn't sink, but lay bobbing on the surface and the algae, displaced by its fall, reformed around it. Anthony felt the sour taste of this green, elemental weed on his tongue and vomited into the mud. Out of his mouth came pouring the chewed and mangled pieces of the body of Christ.

Olivia's murder, when it became known, caught the public interest for some time. 'Why?' the people asked. '*Why did he kill her?*' But after the trial, it was quite soon forgotten. Even the question *why*, never answered to counsel's satisfaction, was forgotten and Anthony started on his six year prison sentence in the same way as he had started on his Priory retreat – with a frail kind of hope.

God, however, did seem to have left him, and the only feelings of wonder he ever experienced again were on windy days. He taught some of his prison colleagues how to make kites out of coat-hanger wire, newspaper and paste, and when the wind bellowed round the prison walls, these things could be seen dancing above the exercise yard. In the tug of their strings, Anthony could feel the pull of heaven.

The Bellows of the Fire

THE TWO THINGS I cared about most in the world until this morning were my dog, Whisper, and the bungalow under the viaduct.

Whisper is black and white with black blobs round her eyes and my aunt Nellie Miller says she reminds her of a panda.

Whisper is a one-person panda. The one person she loves is me. She waits for me to get home from school with her nose in the letter-box flap.

The viaduct is about a mile from our house. In winter, I can't get to it before dark, but in summer I take Whisper there every day. Trains used to go over it, but the railway line was torn up before I was born, so I've always known it like it is now, which is like a roof garden of weeds.

On rainy days, I hardly stop on the viaduct to look at the bungalow, because down there in the mist and drizzle it looks a bit sorry for itself. But in the sunshine, you see that it isn't sorry for itself at all and that the people who live there give it so much love and attention, you can't imagine they've got time for normal life.

Despite what's happened and what may happen in the future, I still feel that if that bungalow was mine, I'd be one of the happiest people in Devon. The only thing I'd add to the garden would be a wall all round it to keep Whisper in, so that she couldn't roam off to the sea when I wasn't there and drown.

The sea's second on my list of places I like, except that

the sea does something to me: it makes me long for things. I sit down on the beach and stare out at invisible France, and this feeling of longing makes me dreamy as a fish. One of the things I long for is for time to pass.

It was my fourteenth birthday last week. We don't seem to celebrate my birthday in our family any more and I think this is because my mother says it only reminds her how fast her life is slipping away.

The only birthday I remember well is when I was six. My mother still considered herself young then and we had a new car and we drove to Dartmoor. The plan was, we were going to make a fire and cook sausages in it. I thought this was the best idea my parents had ever had.

But in the car, on the way to Dartmoor, my brothers bagged all the good jobs in advance. 'Bags collect the wood.' 'Bags light the fire.' 'Bags be in charge of cooking.' Only after a long time did my mother remember me and say, 'What about you, Susan? What job are you going to do, dear?' I didn't know what other jobs there were. 'She can't do anything, she's too little,' said my brothers.

We drove for ages in silence, but then my father had an idea. 'You can be the bellows of the fire, Susie. That means you have to blow on it and your breath keeps it going.' This didn't seem like a nice job to me. Blowing out cake candles was horrible enough. So I thought, I'm not going to breathe on their fire. I'm going to be absolutely quiet and hardly breathe at all. I'm going to be as silent as a stone.

Since then – or perhaps always, I don't know – I've been very quiet in my family. I notice things about them, like how they all love noise and seem to believe that happiness is *in* noise somewhere and that misery is in silence. They think that I'm a miserable person. What I think is that there are millions of things they'll never understand.

Our house is a modern house in a terrace of identical ones. Noise and mess from these houses spills out all over the puny little gardens and all over the street. If you were a visitor from France or somewhere and you thought all of Britain was like our terrace, you'd say it was the most hideous country in the world. Getting away from our house is something I think about every day of my life. My brothers are trying to get work in this town. They're trying to get jobs, so they can stay on and live in houses like these ones, or worse. And girls I know at school, that's what they want too. They want to be beauticians or hairdressers in the crappy shopping arcade. If I thought that was going to happen to me, I'd drown myself.

I took Whisper to the sea this evening. I throw things into the waves and she gets them out. She's terrific at this, much better than other dogs we see. Then we lay in the sun while her coat dried and I told her the news that came this morning.

I like secrets. I'm going to keep this one as long as I can. It'll come out eventually, though, and then my mother will say, '*Film*, Susan? What film?' And I will have to tell her the story.

It's a story about a community. It's set in a town like ours, not far from the coast. It's based on something which actually happened, on a person who actually lived, a girl called Julie who was fourteen and a fire raiser. She was a Girl Guide and her Dad worked for the town council. These things were important in the story, because the places where she started the fires were the places where new things were getting done, like a new Leisure Centre was being built and a new Bingo Palace.

Being a Girl Guide, she knew how to start fires without matches or paraffin or anything, so there was never any evidence left lying about, and this is why it took the police ages and ages to track Julie down. And also, they decided all the wrong things to start with. They decided the fires were started by a person from an ethnic minority, who resented the clubs and places where he wasn't welcome, so all they were really looking for were young Indians or West Indian youths. It took them a year before they suspected the daughter of a town councillor, and by that time, seven fires had been raised and the Bingo Palace had burned to the ground. She was caught in the end only because she set fire to the Girl Guide hut.

So, anyway, the thing is, they're making a film about her. The TV company came down here months ago. They arranged auditions in all the schools. All they said was, you had to be about fourteen and interested in acting. I haven't been in many school plays. When we did *The Insect Play*, I was only a moth with nothing to say. But I am very interested in acting, because in the last year I've realised that what I do all the time at home is *act*. I act the sort of person my family think I am, with nothing to say for herself and no opinions on anything, when inside me I'm not like that at all, I just don't let my opinions out. I'd rather save my breath. I plan, though. At school with one or two of the teachers and then on my walks with Whisper to the viaduct and the sea, I plan a proper life.

Not that many people from our school went to the auditions. They thought it was going to be too hard, and anything that seems hard to them, they let it go. But it wasn't difficult. You had five minutes to look at the script and then you had to read out a speech from near the end of the film, where they ask Julie why she started the fires, and she tells them. She tells them what she feels about communities like this one. She despises them. She thinks they've been hypnotised and corrupted. She thinks greed is all they understand.

It was quite a long, angry speech. When it came to my turn to read it, I pretended I was saying it all to my brothers and that they didn't understand a word of it and the more confused they looked, the more angrily the words came out. When I ended it, I knew I'd made an impression on the person who had asked me to read it. He was staring at me in amazement and then he said would I be able to come down to London in July for a second audition, which would be in front of a camera.

In the letter that came this morning, they told me that over two hundred girls had been seen for the part of Julie and that now there are just six of us. And us six will go to London – not all together, but each of us on a different day – and we will all pretend to be Julie, the arsonist, and other real actors will pretend to be her Mum and Dad and everyone and they'll decide at the end of all that who they're going to cast.

When I think about this now, I realise that although I've

longed to get away from this town and longed to be the owner of the bungalow under the viaduct, I've never before longed for anything I could actually have, *now*. Getting away and living in that little house were all way-into-the-future kinds of things, but this, this part in the film is waiting for someone now, this year, now, and I've got a one-in-six chance of getting it and I want to get it so badly that it's been impossible, since this morning, to concentrate on lessons or eat a shitty school dinner because what I could feel all the time was my heart beating.

The only time I could feel calmer about it was on my walk with Whisper. What I told myself then was that I have had years of 'acting experience' at home and probably those other five girls have had none and what you see and hear of them is all there is. But me, I've been saving my breath. Saving it up for now.

When we walked back, by the time we got to the viaduct, I'd made myself believe – and I'm going to stick to this – that I am definitely the right person for this part and that the TV people are intelligent enough to recognise this and to offer it to me. And when I get it, that's going to be something.

But I still, to be on the safe side, looked for a long time at the bungalow under the viaduct and told myself that if you know how and where to look for them, there are loads of different ways you can be happy. Being an actress is one. Having a nice home in a place where there's silence is another. You just have to work at it all, slowly and carefully, like Dad made that fire catch on Dartmoor in the rain, one stick at a time.

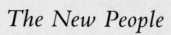

The New People

M ILLICENT GRAVES IS leaving.
   Today, with her friend and companion, Alison
Prout, she has been for her last walk to the village and
back. She has sat for a while on a wooden seat under the
war memorial. The ice-cream van, playing four bars of a
tune she thought was called 'The Happy Wanderer', drew
up by the war memorial and obscured her view of the
village green, the pub, the bank and the co-op. A few kids
queued up at the van's window. Millicent Graves, who
had heard on Radio 4 that some ice-cream men were also
drug traders, stared at the children. They were pale and
obese. Millicent Graves imagined that inside their skulls
was confusion and darkness.

   Upstairs now Alison Prout is packing clothes. The
clothes are Millicent's. There are hats and furs, unworn for
thirty years but preserved in boxes with mothballs and
tissue paper. There is a black lace ballgown and a black
velvet 'theatre dress'. There are white kid gloves and
oyster-coloured stockings. Millicent can remember the
feel of these ancient clothes against her skin. She has told
Alison to pack them all – even the black lace gown and a
hat with ostrich plumes – because she wants to believe that
in her new life there will be the time and the climate for a
little eccentricity. She can see herself in the old feathered
hat, perfect for keeping the hot sun off her head. She
might, she has decided, go shopping in it and enjoy watching the shopkeepers' faces as out from its ridiculous shade

comes her order for half a kilo of parmesan. Or it might become a gardening hat, in which case it will be the nuns who spy her on the other side of their wall – a small but striking figure in her new landscape, going round with the watering can, placing cool stones on the clematis root. Alison Prout has had a bitter argument with Millicent on the subject of the clothes, certain as she is that Millicent's motive for taking them is detestable vanity. Millicent was, long ago, beautiful. Now, she is, simply, old. But the clothes, the foolish, expensive clothes, are a reminder – another among many reminders – of her power. And that power, Alison admits to herself as she folds and sorts her friend's possessions, is not yet completely spent.

In a week's time, Millicent and Alison, who have lived together in the cottage for nineteen years, will have left it for ever and The New People will have moved in.

It is a summer afternoon and the light on the garden is beguiling, Alison thinks, as she passes and re-passes the small bedroom window, carrying Millicent's things. Millicent is downstairs, dusting the weasel. She has promised Alison that she will 'make a start on the books'. There are more than two thousand of these. When The New People first arrived to look round the cottage they appeared genuinely afraid at the sight of them. They'd imagined thick walls, perhaps, but not this extra insulation of literature. Then, as Millicent led them on into the sitting room and they noticed the stuffed weasel under its glass cloche, their fear palpably increased, as if the long-dead animal was going to dart at their ankle veins. And yet they didn't retreat. They knew the weasel would be leaving with the women; their glances said, 'We can take down all these book shelves'. As they left, they muttered, 'We shall be instructing the agents . . .'

After they'd gone, Alison had started to cry. 'They'll change it all,' she sobbed, 'I always imagined people like us would buy it.' Millicent reprimanded her. 'Change is good,' she said fiercely, 'and anyway, dear, there are no more people like us.'

But later that evening, Millicent found that she too was looking at the shape and detail of rooms and wondering how they would be altered. After supper, she'd gone out into the garden and stared at the summer night and thought, they will never see it as I see it, those New People, because even if their hands don't change it, their minds will. 'We've got ghosts now!' she announced to Alison as she went in. 'Ghosts who come before instead of after.'

Now, polishing the weasel, Millicent senses that the ghosts are with her in the sitting room. She turns round. 'What we don't understand,' they say, 'is why you're going.'

'Ah,' says Millicent.

Then she notices that Alison has crept down from sorting the old clothes and is sitting in an armchair, saying nothing.

'Is it a long story?'

'No,' says Millicent. 'I'm going because I've been replaced. I look around, in very many places where I once was and now I not only do not see myself there, I see no one who ever resembled me. It's as if I have been obliterated. And I can't, at the age of sixty-nine, accept my obliteration, so I am simply going somewhere where I shall be visible again, at least to myself.'

The New People look utterly perplexed. They want to say, 'We knew you literary folk were a bit mad, a bit touched, but we thought you tried to make sense to ordinary people. We thought this was common courtesy.'

'No,' snaps Millicent, reading their minds, 'it is not common courtesy, yet what I am saying is tediously simple.'

'Well, I'm afraid we don't understand it.'

'Of course you don't. Of course you don't . . .' Millicent mumbles.

'What you still haven't told us,' say The New People, trying to drag the conversation onto a solid foundation, 'is where you're actually going.'

Millicent looks at Alison. Alison turns her face towards the window and the afternoon sun shines on her hair, which is still reddish and only dulled a little with grey.

'Umbria,' says Millicent.

'Sorry?' say The New People.

'Yes. The house we're buying is by a convent wall. It belonged to the nuns for centuries. It was a place where important guests were put. Now, we shall be the "guests".'

At this point, The New People get up. They say they have to leave. They say they have a great friend who's mad on Italian food and who is starting a local Foodie Society. 'Tonight,' they laugh, 'is the inaugural nosebag!'

Millicent turns away from them and goes back to her polishing. When she looks round again, she finds they've gone.

'They've gone!' she calls to Alison, who is after all upstairs and not sitting silently in a chair.

'What, Millie? Who've gone?'

'Those people,' says Millicent, 'those ghosts. For the time being.'

At supper in the kitchen, Alison says: 'I think I'm going to try not to think about The New People, and if I was you, I'd try not to think about them either.'

'What a very complicated construction that is, Alison,' says Millicent, helping herself to the raspberries she picked a few moments ago in the dusk.

'Particularly tomorrow evening,' says Alison.

'Why particularly tomorrow evening?'

'While I'm out.'

'Out? Where are you going?'

'To say goodbye to Diana.'

'I see,' says Millicent. 'Well, it is going to be extremely difficult *not* to think about them, because they will be here.'

'They're only here in your mind, Millie.'

'I mean, they will actually *be here*. They're bringing a builder.'

'Tomorrow evening?'

'Yes. They're driving down from London.'

'Oh. Then I won't go out.'

'That would be considerate.'

'On the other hand, I promised Diana . . .'

142

'I marvel that you feel an emotional goodbye to be necessary.'

'Not "emotional".'

'In fact, why not, when we get to Italy, just send a postcard?'

'As if we were on holiday, I suppose you mean.'

Millicent sniffs. Another thing she hopes of her future life is that Alison, fifty next year, will have no more love affairs. She's never expressed this hope, except in her recent poetry, which, as once-praising, now-contemptuous critics have noted, is all about betrayal. She hadn't realised that betrayal was so unfashionable a subject nor indeed that her poems were 'all about' it. Perhaps, she decides capriciously, she will ask The New People about these things and watch their moons of faces closely to see whether or not they understand the words.

They arrive at seven. Alison has promised to be back by seven-thirty. On entering the cottage, they say, God, they're sorry, but since their last visit someone has told them that she, Millicent Graves, is quite a famous poetess and it's awful to say they'd never heard of her.

'Oh, I see,' says Millicent. 'Then why did you say you thought literary people were mad?'

'I beg your pardon?' they say.

'You said you knew that literary folk were a bit touched . . .'

'We said that?'

'Or did I imagine it?'

'You imagined it. You must have done.'

They introduce the builder. He doesn't look, to Millicent Graves, like a builder, but more like a town councillor, wearing a brown suit and brogues. 'Perhaps you're a New Builder?' she asks. The man frowns and tugs out a pipe. He says he's been in the construction business half a lifetime. 'I think,' says Millicent, as she pictures Alison arriving at Diana's house and being greeted with a kiss, 'that everything's become very different and confusing.'

She leads them in. As they reach the sitting room, and the builder starts to look up at the bowed ceiling beams and to prod the springy, flaking plaster of the walls,

143

Millicent finds she can't remember the name of The New People and wonders in fact whether she's ever known it.

'Oh, Prue and Simon,' they tell her.

Yes, she wants to say, but the surname? What was that? Something like Haydock-Park, wasn't it, or is that a Grand Prix circuit or a racecourse? She asks the New Builder his name. 'Jack Silverstone,' he announces impatiently.

'Lord!' exclaims Millicent. 'Everybody's careering about.'

The New People glance at each other. We must obliterate every trace of her, says this fearful look. And Jack Silverstone nods, as if in reassurance: It can all be changed. You won't know it's the same house. It's going to cost a bit, that's all.

'Where do you want to start?' asks Millicent.

'Oh . . .' says Prue.

'Well . . .' says Simon.

'Upstairs,' says Jack Silverstone.

So now, as Millicent gets out the sherry bottle from Alison's tidy kitchen cupboard, they're up above her head in the bathroom. Conversations, in timber-framed houses, escape as easily as heat through the floors and Millicent can hear Prue say to Jack Silverstone: 'This is the one drawback, Jack.' And it appears that Prue wants two bathrooms. Though they will only use the cottage at weekends, she feels, 'It simply isn't viable with one.'

'What about downstairs?' asks Jack Silverstone.

'Downstairs?'

'The little room next to the kitchen.'

'Her study? Convert that into a second bathroom?'

'Why not? Got no use for a study, have you?'

'Simon?'

'Good God, no. Don't plan to bring work here. Need a phone, that's all.'

They start to clatter towards the stairs. Now they'll come down and go into the study, where nothing has ever been disturbed but only moved about gently to accommodate the hoover, and start a conversation about piping.

Millicent leaves the sherry unpoured and marches

quickly to the desk where all the unfashionable words on the subject of dereliction have been set down and picks up the telephone. By the time The New People have opened her door and exclaimed with barely concealed annoyance at finding her there, she has dialled Diana's number and has begun to wonder whereabouts in Diana's very beautiful house Alison may be standing or sitting or even lying down, because although it is now 7.25 by the silent study clock, Millicent is certain that Alison is still there and that unless summoned immediately she will come home very late, long after The New People have gone, leaving Millicent alone with the darkness and the ghosts.

The telephone rings and isn't answered. The New People have retreated to the kitchen where impatiently in their minds they are tearing Millicent's old cupboards off the walls.

'So tell us why you're going. Won't you?' say The New People, sipping sherry.

'Well,' says Millicent, 'I'll tell you a story, if you like.'

'A story?'

'Yes. And it's this. Men have never been particularly important to me, but one man was and that was my father. He was a scientist. All his early work was in immunology. But then he became very interested in behaviours, animal behaviour and then human behaviours. And from this time, our family life was quite changed, because he started bringing to his laboratory and then into the house all kinds of strangers. They would mostly be very unhappy people and their unhappiness and noise made it impossible for us to live as we'd once lived and everything we valued – silence, for instance, and little jokes that only we as a family understood – had disappeared for ever. And then my youngest sister, Christina, whom I loved very very much, committed suicide. So you see. Sometimes one has to act.'

Three faces, turned in expectation towards Millicent, turn away.

'Dreadful story,' mumbles Prue.

'Can we have a look at the study now?' says Jack Silverstone.

145

'Yes,' says Millicent. 'My study in Italy overlooks the nuns' vegetable garden. They told me they hoe in silence, but I expect from time to time one might hear them murmuring, don't you think?'

They don't know how to reply. In the study, they whisper. They've understood now how their plans can be overheard.

Millicent pours herself more sherry and notices that, as she predicted, Alison is not home and that the sun has gone down behind the laurels.

The New People emerge, beaming. Clearly, they have decided where the lavatory can go and where the bath. Millicent fills their glasses. 'The convent is, of course, crumbling,' she tells them, 'that's why the nuns have been forced to sell off the guest house – to try to repair the fabric. The Church in Italy used to hold people in their blood. Prayer was food. But it isn't like that any more. It's in decay, and all over the place there are empty churches and the old plaster saints have been replaced by plastic things.'

'There's a lot of shoddy muck about,' says Jack Silverstone, 'take my trade . . .'

'One imagines that perhaps certain African or South American Indian tribes are held to certain ways and certain places in their blood, but I think no one else is, do you? Certainly not in this country, unless it's an individual held to another individual by love. What do you think?'

'Well,' says Prue.

'Time,' says Simon.

'Time?' says Millicent.

'Yes. If you're in something like Commodities, as I am, you don't have the time for any other commitments.'

'And as for the Church,' says Jack Silverstone, 'all that ever was was bloodthirsty.'

At this moment, Millicent hears the sound of Alison's car. It's eight thirty-five. The New People get up and thank Millicent for the sherry and tell her they've seen everything they needed to see.

Alison looks white. Her straight, small mouth is set into an even straighter, smaller line. Millicent decides to ignore

– at least for the time being – the set of Alison's mouth and tells her friend with a smile: 'They're called the Haydock-Parks!'

'No, they are *not*, Millicent,' snaps Alison. 'Why do you always have to get names wrong?'

'What are they called, then?'

'The Hammond-Clarks.'

'Oh well, the builder is called Silverstone.'

'I very much doubt it.'

'You always doubted a great deal that was true, dear. He is called Silverstone, and I shall from now on refer to these people as the Haydock-Parks because it suits them extremely well.'

Alison goes angrily up the stairs and into her room. The door closes. Her anger, Millicent notices, has made the house throb. She wonders how many times and in what degree the timbers and the lathes have shifted, over all the years, to the violent commotions of their friendship. She ponders the origin of the phrase 'brought the house down' and wonders if it was originally applied to anger and not to laughter. How splendid if, as their removal van drove away, the house gave one final shudder of release and collapsed in a pile of sticks at The New People's feet.

She waits for a while for Alison to come down. She's hungry, but she refuses to eat supper alone.

She goes out into the garden and folds up the two deck chairs. 'Order before night' was a favourite saying of her father's, and before he started imposing a more or less perpetual state of disorder on their previously calm and prospering household, he would, each evening, observe his own strict ritual of collecting every toy scattered round the house and garden and returning it to its place in the nursery, before checking that all the downstairs windows were shut, the curtains drawn, the silver cupboard locked, the backgammon board closed, the lights extinguished and the eiderdowns in place over the bodies of his sleeping daughters. Millicent remembers that Christina once admitted to her that she would often let her eiderdown slip onto the floor on purpose and lie awake waiting for this infinitely comforting moment when it would be lifted gently from the floor and placed over her. When the strangers kept arriving, there was no time in her father's life for 'order before night'; there was, as Millicent remembers it, simply night. It descended swiftly. Patiently, the family waited for dawn, but it never came. Christina died. Millicent retreated from death by starting to write poetry.

She hadn't expected fame. It had come as suddenly and as unexpectedly as the arrival of the strangers. And it had changed her, made her bold, excited and free. Other people complained about it; Millicent Graves always found it an absorbing companion. Now, she misses it. Her frail hope is that in Italy she will miss it less. It still astonishes her that work once so highly valued can now be so utterly forgotten.

She props up the deckchairs in the porch. In the distance, she hears the church clock chime the three-quarter hour. The evening is warm. She wonders how often and for how long the convent tolls its massive bells and whether these summonses will help to structure a future which she knows she hasn't imagined fully enough. Alison has expressed anxiety about the bells, complaining that the days will seem long enough without being woken at dawn.

Resigned to an evening alone, Millicent makes a salad and eats it. She supposes that Alison is sleeping, but then when the telephone rings, it's answered upstairs. Tiptoeing to the sitting room, Millicent can hear Alison talking in halting sentences, as if she's trying not to cry. Millicent sniffs. 'I'm much too old for all this!' she says aloud.

In the night, the ghosts of The New People come into Millicent's room and tear off her wallpaper and replace her old velvet curtains with something called a festoon blind, that draws upwards into big bunches of fabric, like pairs of knickers.

'I see,' says Millicent.

They don't say anything. They're standing back and admiring the window.

'We used to wear cotton knickers like that,' Millicent tells them. 'I never saw my own, not from any provoca-

148

tive angle, but I used to see Elizabeth's and Christina's when we were invited to parties and they would bend down to do up their shoes, and I used to think that the backs of girls' legs looked very strong and lovely.'

The New People are utterly silent and satisfied and fulfilled by the curtains and have drifted off into a contented sleep with the festoons falling caressingly about their heads.

'Night in this cottage,' Millicent whispers, knowing that nothing she says will wake them, 'is usually kind because it's quiet. I've found that in this quiet, I've often started to understand things which may not have been plain to me during the day.

'It was during one particular night, very, very cold, with that bitter feeling of snow to come, that I decided I couldn't endure it, the unloveliness of England, I just couldn't stand it any more, its comatose people, its ravaged landscape. Because we're in a dark age, that's what I think. But no one listens to what I think any more. Millicent Graves is out of fashion, passé, past, part of what once was, a voice we no longer hear.

'So I decided I would go. It seemed, from that night, inevitable. And you see where I've put myself? Slap up against a convent wall! But do you know why I'm able to do that? Because the wall itself, which I believed was so strong, so much more substantial than anything we have left in this brutal-minded country, the wall itself is crumbling! The money I've paid for my little house will prop it up for a bit, but I don't think it will rebuild it, and the best I can hope for is that it doesn't collapse on my head – not till I'm buried, at least.'

At this mention of burial, Millicent sees The New People open their eyes and listen and she thinks she knows why they look so startled: the thought has popped into their minds that despite all the extensive re-planning and re-decorating they're going to do, traces of Millicent's habitation may still remain in the house to disturb them. They imagine how they might be made aware of her. They're giving a dinner party, say. Friends of Simon's from the City will have driven down with their wives, and

149

suddenly Prue or Simon will remember that even the walls of the dining-room used to be lined with books, and the flow of their conversation, which is as easy for them as the flow of money, will be halted – just for a moment – because one of them, searching for a word or phrase, understands for a second that there are thousands of words they will never use or even know and remembers that access to these words was once here, in the very room, and is now lost. The moment passes. It's all right. But Simon and Prue both separately wonder, why is it not possible never to think of her?

'Good!' says Millicent aloud. 'That's something, at least, their little discomfort.'

She has gone to sleep and is dreaming of Italy when she's woken by Alison's gentle tap on her door. This knocking on each other's doors is a courtesy neither would want to break; it allows them to share their life without any fear of trespass.

Millicent puts on her light and Alison comes in and sits down on the end of her bed. 'I couldn't sleep, Millie,' she says, 'I think we have to talk.'

'Yes, dear,' says Millicent.

Millicent decides to put on her glasses, so that she can see Alison clearly. Dishonesty must not be allowed to slip past her because dishonesty she can never forgive. She watches Alison's breasts rise as she takes a big breath and says with great sadness: 'I'm not certain that I can go to Italy with you. I think that, for the moment, it's not possible for me to go.'

Millicent blinks. Her eyes were always like a bird's eyes, hooded above and beneath.

'Diana, I suppose.'

'Partly so.'

'And the other part?'

Alison's eyes have been turned away from Millicent until now, but as she speaks, she looks up into her face.

'I can't,' she says, 'feel all the pessimism you feel. Don't think I'm being harsh, Millie, when I say that I feel that some of it comes not from the way our world has

150

changed, but from the way *you've* changed – from being so very beautiful and praised, to being . . .'

'Old and despised.'

'That's how you choose to see it. I don't think anyone despises you. They've just learned, over the years, to disagree with you sometimes and not praise everything you write.'

'They don't praise any of it, Alison. They want me to be quiet.'

'Well, again, that's how you've decided to see it.'

'No. They do. But that's not what you've come to discuss. I suppose it's Diana's beauty, is it? You're infatuated.'

'I may be. What I find I can't believe when I'm with her is that this country has lost all the good things it had. I know it's lost some of them, but I don't believe it's "finished", as you say it is. I just can't believe that, Millie. I can't. And I know that if I go to Italy, I'm going to miss it. I'm going to be homesick for England.'

'What for?' says Millicent indignantly. 'For riots? For waste? For greed? For turkeyburgers?'

'Of course not.'

'Then for what? For this garden, maybe. Or Diana's garden. But what are English gardens, dear? They're fragile oases, preserved by one thing and one thing only: money. And when the economy falters, as falter it undoubtedly will, all your peace of mind – that keeps you in the garden and other people outside it, suffering in those concrete estates – will vanish. Then what joy or satisfaction will you get from the garden?'

'I can't believe it will come to that.'

'It's coming, Alison. Do you know what the Haydock-Parks are going to put in before anything else? A burglar alarm.'

'I know all that. But there are so very many decent people, Millie, who want the country to survive, who want to make things better . . .'

'Decent people? Who? Name one decent person.'

'The kind of people we've always known . . .'

'Our friends? I don't think they're "decent", Alison. I

think they're infinitely corruptible and infinitely weak, and when it comes to saving England, the task simply isn't going to fall to them, it's going to fall to people like the Haydock-Parks, The New People, and what kind of 'salvation' do you ever imagine that's going to be?'

Alison is silent. When she thinks about it, she is perfectly happy to let Millicent win the argument. What she will not let her do is change her mind.

The silence endures. Alison picks at the fringe of her dressing-gown cord. Millicent takes off her glasses and rubs her eyes.

'I have never,' says Millicent after a while, 'been at all good at being quite and utterly alone. How in the world do you think I'm going to get on in that Italian house without you?'

'I really don't know, Millie,' says Alison sadly, 'I expect I shall worry about you a great deal.'

Refusing to think about Alison after she has gone back to her own room, Millicent snaps out the light and lies on her back and sees the dawn starting to frame the curtains. Just outside her window is a clump of tall hazel bushes. Pigeons have roosted in these trees for as long as Millicent can remember and she thinks now that if she's going to miss one thing, it will be the murmuring of these birds.

They lull her to sleep. She dreams her dead sister, Christina, comes and stands by her bed and puts her child's hand on Millicent's grey head. 'I am wearing,' Christina announces solemnly, 'the Haydock-Parks' curtains, just to mess them up, and in a few moments I'm going to drink this little phial of White Arsenic I've stolen from father's lab, and it will make me die.'

'Don't die, Christina,' Millicent begs, 'dear Christina . . .'

'Oh no, I'm definitely going to die,' says Christina, 'because I think loss is the saddest thing anyone could possibly imagine. Don't you, Millie? I think losing something you once had is the most unbearable thing of all. Don't you?'

'What have you lost, Christina? I'll find it again for you.

I'll get it back, whatever it was. Just as long as you don't die . . .'

'No. You can't get it back. Thank you for offering, Millie, but I know that what we once had in this house went away when the strangers arrived and even if mother pleaded and begged and *made* father send them away, I know that they damaged us, damaged our love, and however hard we tried to get it for ourselves again, we never ever could.'

This dream is so sad that Millicent has to wake herself up, even though she knows that her old head which her fifteen-year-old sister was touching is very tired and in need of sleep.

Thoughts of Christina and of death linger with her. She feels, as she has never felt before, afraid not so much of death, but, in dying, of yielding territory to others who may desecrate and destroy the few things which have seemed precious to her and which, in the absence of any belief in God, have been part of a code by which she's tried to live.

In Italy, she promises her new hosts, the nuns, she will alter nothing in their house, nothing fundamental, and to the land around it she will behave kindly. But when she dies, what will happen to it? Who will come next? Which strangers?

'Probably,' she says aloud to the pigeons, 'it's wiser to own no territory at all and just be like that man in my Samuel Palmer print, who lies down alone in the landscape with his book.'

Next door, she hears Alison get up.

'Daybreak,' announces Millicent.